Topeka Atchison

Texas Coast Country

also briefly describing the resources of all counties along the Gulf,

Colorado & Santa Fe railway line

Topeka Atchison

Texas Coast Country
also briefly describing the resources of all counties along the Gulf, Colorado & Santa Fe railway line

ISBN/EAN: 9783337238759

Printed in Europe, USA, Canada, Australia, Japan

Cover: Foto ©Andreas Hilbeck / pixelio.de

More available books at **www.hansebooks.com**

Texas
Coast
Country

.* .* .*

Also briefly describing
the Resources of all
Counties along the
Gulf, Colorado & Santa fe
Railway line

Issued by the Passenger Department
Santa fe Route
May, 1898

70009

Corbitt & Butterfield Co.,
Railway Printers,
Chicago.

Somewhat Personal

· ·

DO you live in a climate where the winters are long and severe? In Texas there is practically no winter; one can comfortably work outdoors the year round.

Is your locality subject to devastating drouths? In the Coast Country of Texas the average rainfall is forty-five inches a year, well distributed through the growing season ; and no irrigation is required.

Is the soil of your farm worn out? Texas soil rarely requires fertilizers; it is deep and rich and permanent.

Does it require all you earn for living expenses? The cost is 40% less to build a house in Texas than in the North, 50% less for clothing, and 80% less for fuel.

Are you now restricted to one main crop a year? Along the Gulf Coast of Texas a man can raise two or three crops of vegetables and alfalfa per annum, and more than one crop of some other staples; a great diversity is also possible.

Are you interested in horticulture? Texas fruit lands annually pay $200 to $500 net per acre. The fruit season begins early and lasts to a late date.

Is your northern farm worth $100 an acre, with a high tax rate and low prices for products? Why not try the $10 an acre lands in the southern part of Texas, where taxes are low and markets excellent?

This pamphlet is intended for the man desirous of more information on the important subject of where to go for a new home. The descriptions are limited to the southern portion of Texas, along the Gulf

Coast, with a little information about other sections on the Gulf, Colorado & Santa Fe Railway. Farmers, fruit-raisers and land-owners are permitted to speak for themselves. The unsigned articles have been compiled from the most reliable sources.

Here is a country which it is believed offers ample rewards for well-directed toil; where the homeseeker may find cheap land, abundant crops, good markets, a friendly climate and hospitable neighbors.

If, after reading what is herein contained, you are sufficiently interested to wish to investigate further by taking a trip to Texas and seeing for yourself, remember that the Santa Fe Route is the direct line from Chicago, Kansas City, Denver and other northern and eastern points to the heart of the Coast Country. For full particulars respecting train service, ticket rates, etc., confer with any ticket agent or address the undersigned.

W. J. BLACK, General Passenger Agent,
Atchison, Topeka & Santa Fe Ry.,
TOPEKA, KANSAS.

C. A. HIGGINS, Ass't Gen'l Passenger Agent,
Atchison, Topeka & Santa Fe Ry.,
CHICAGO.

W. S. KEENAN, General Passenger Agent,
Gulf, Colorado & Santa Fe Ry.,
GALVESTON, TEXAS

Facts About Texas

• • •

Texas is the biggest State in the Union. Texans themselves, who ought to know if anybody does, claim it is the *best* State. Without arguing a point that has the unanimous assent of nearly three millions of people, it would be strange indeed if an empire five times larger than England and out of which could be carved four New Englands, did not rank first in other respects than mere size.

Its Rank Texas wears the blue ribbon in regard to area, production of cotton, number of sheep, cattle and horses raised; amount of funds set apart for free public schools and colleges, and the size and finish of the beautiful capitol building at Austin. It ranks fourth in wealth, about third in railroad mileage, and seventh in population.

A Comparison Texas produces more rice than South Carolina, more sugar and sorghum than Louisiana, more wheat than the Dakotas; has more prairie land than Kansas, a larger coal area than Pennsylvania, greater oak forests than West Virginia, more corn land than Illinois; raises more cotton than Mississippi; is capable of producing more iron ore than Alabama, and excels New Hampshire in its granite.

Its Area The Lone Star State extends from the 26th to the 36th parallel of latitude and lies between the 94th and 97th degrees of longitude. The average length, east and west, is 800 miles, and average breadth, north and south, 750 miles. It possesses 400 miles of coast line; has navigable rivers equaling those of any five other states, and 8,952 miles of railroad, mostly trunk lines. From Texarkana to El Paso equals the distance from New York to Chicago. A man bicycling on its boundary lines would travel over 4,000 miles. There are 265,780 square miles of "room," and hardly ten people yet to each square mile. The Austrian empire, with about the same area, sustains a population of 36,000,000; the German empire, with less area, has more than 50,000,000 inhabitants. Texas could sustain in prosperity a population of 95,000,000. A recent census shows that 255,000 farmers cultivate their own land, 95,000 are tenants, and 56,000 day laborers. Disciples of calamity are not numerous in Texas.

Topography Beginning with a level coast, there is a gradual ascent north and west, to an elevation of 4,000 feet, which affords excellent drainage. Three-fourths of this vast area can be profitably cultivated. The southeastern and southern sections are level and free from rock—this is the famous fruit belt, rivaling California. Dense forests of oak, elm, hickory and pine cover the eastern district—there being 25,000,000 acres of

A VOYAGE DOWN CHOCOLATE BAYOU

merchantable pine alone. The center of Texas is an undulating prairie, like the prolific plains of Kansas, with succulent grasses—a fine stock country and capable of raising immense crops of corn, wheat and cotton. West Texas is broken by hills and mountains, with fertile valleys. The Panhandle region is a table-land, and noted for its fat cattle.

Soils As a rule the rich, deep soil of Texas needs no fertilizer for standard crops. A moderate top-dressing of cotton-seed helps to make

a larger crop, but is not absolutely required. Anything can be raised that grows in the temperate zone.
Sugar cane, cotton, figs, olives, pears and grapes are
a remarkable success in the South. The Mediter-
ranean countries do not excel the Texas Coast
Country in raising fruit.

Texas furnishes its citizens a good living.

Products In 1895 the various products of
this State (from fields, gardens,
orchards, ranches and factories) amounted to a
princely fortune. The values of the leading crops
were: cotton and cotton seed, $55,500,000; corn,
$23,500,000; wheat, $625,000; oats, $3,165,000;
garden produce, $2,850,000; potatoes, $1,000,000;
hay, $1,335,000; sugar cane, molasses and sorghum,
$2,100,000; peaches, apples, grapes, plums, pears
and melons, $1,500,000; millet, barley and rye,
$735,000.

Texas ranks seventh as a corn producing state,
first in sheep, eighth in hogs, and her herds of
cattle are one-sixth of the entire number in the
United States.

And that is not the whole story.

In 1897 live stock was assessed at $78,365,500, the
leading items being horses and mules, cattle, sheep
and hogs. Even the despised goat is quoted at a
quarter of a million "simoleons."

Schools, etc. Material wealth is not all.
Texas has accumulated a per-
manent school fund of over $17,000,000. During
1896-97, 10,644 white and 2,821 colored teachers
were employed. Land Commissioner Baker reports
38,000,000 acres of land surveyed for the permanent
school fund. All prominent religious denominations
are well represented by thriving churches, and
society in general is of the highest order. The
hospitality of Texas is proverbial; the latch-string
is always out.

Resources What is dug out of the ground
must not be forgotten. Coal and
iron are plentiful; one bituminous coal formation
on the Red River covers 12,000 square miles, with
seams three feet in thickness. Bituminous and lignite coals are mined in the Nueces district, along the
Rio Grande River. Extensive deposits of iron are

reported to exist in eastern Texas, covering 1,000 square miles of surface, many veins being ten feet thick. There are surface indications of petroleum in several counties along the eastern border, and paying wells have been sunk at Nacogdoches. Besides these three fields of iron, three of coal and three of oil, three distinct districts of copper have been opened up—the ores of the trans-Pecos region being extensively worked. Gold and silver mines have been discovered near El Paso, and a 140-foot bed of rock salt underlies Victoria. Gypsum occurs in the Abilene Country. Asphaltum, bat guano,

"A LITTLE FARM, WELL TILLED."

marls, mica and granite are found in paying quantities.

The wealth on top of the ground, waiting to be tickled into a laughing harvest by the man with the plow, is what Texas depends upon to attract settlers. And while cotton, corn and wheat are the "standbys"—cotton leading in importance—the beautiful region on the Gulf Coast bids fair to soon crowd other sections for first place. Where ten acres will support a family and twenty acres is a competence, the country ought to be thickly populated.

The Coast Country

• • •

Where It Is The Coast region of Texas comprises that part of the State bordering the Gulf of Mexico, from Sabine River to the Rio Grande and extending inland nearly one hundred miles. This pamphlet is more particularly concerned with the portion immediately tributary to the line of the Santa Fe Route, embracing the counties of Harris, Galveston, Brazoria, Ft. Bend, Wharton and Jackson.

It is the location of the coast country that gives to it unequaled advantages and possibilities. Lying on the borders of the temperate and tropic zones, and on the northern shore of a great inland sea, the nipping and eager air of winter and the withering waves of scorching summer heat are not known. There is the gentle, budding springtime, lengthening out into the long days of June; succeeded by summer, Nature's ripening time, which the tradewinds daily sweeping northward from the Gulf temper to a delightful coolness; and then the long, bright, sunny fall, ending with a short, mild winter.

What It Is This is in general a prairie country, an undulating plain, rising five feet to the mile northward from the Gulf, and embracing large forest areas along its water courses. The timber is chiefly oak, live oak, ash, walnut, pecan, mesquite and sycamore. To the west of the Brazos River in the coast country are great tracts of cedar. For several years there has been a large export trade in cedar logs cut far in the interior, hauled to the Brazos and then shipped by boat or rail to Galveston, where they are transhipped to Europe. The general surface is sixty to one hundred feet above mean tide level, most of it sufficiently rolling to afford good drainage into numerous local streams and bayous, which in turn empty into the bays along the great Gulf. Good water for domestic uses is found everywhere under the clay subsoil, and artesian wells are numerous. There are few localities but which can be inexpensively drained and the fertile land thus rendered fit for the plow.

11

Proper drainage is the main problem here—how to get rid of surplus surface water. An underlying stratum of quicksand affords almost perfect sub-irrigation.

The Soil In the river valleys the soil is a deep black, sandy loam. Fertilizers do not seem to be required. There is no "wear out" to it because formed of alluvial deposits originating in the rich lands of the North. The prairie soil consists of three kinds of sandy loam, friable and easily tilled; it rots quicker than the stiffer sod of Illinois or Kansas. It is covered with a very compact sod, that must be broken and allowed to rot before it

GUNNING FOR WILD FOWL ON BUFFALO BAYOU.

can be pulverized and, even then there seems to be something that requires air and heat to rectify before it will produce well. One year's work will bring it into good productive condition, when, with proper fertilizing, it cannot be surpassed. For pears alone this is not necessary, as experience has fully proved that if set on sod that has been simply lapped over with several turns of the plow, the trees will grow about as well as if the ground had been previously prepared.

The black waxy or hog wallow loam (suitable for sugar cane, cotton and berries), is exceedingly rich, though more difficult to till. These soils are no better than those found in the Missouri, Miami,

12

Scioto or Kansas valleys. Their chief value lies in the rare combination which Southern Texas offers of a rich soil, abundant rainfall and genial climate.

The Rainfall

The annual rainfall of the Texas coast district within the rain belt is from 43 to 65 inches, well distributed throughout the spring and summer; besides, the heavy dews, a characteristic feature of the region, furnish a source of daily refreshment for all forms of plant life.

Varied Crops

Both soil and climate are adapted to the bountiful production of a greater variety of field, garden and orchard crops than any like extent of territory in the United States. Indeed, omitting the apple, it is well nigh impossible to mention any field, garden or fruit crop which may not be grown here in the greatest abundance, and of finest quality, if only the right varieties be selected.

Fruits rivaling those of California and vegetables equal to any grown in the North are ready for market here a month to six weeks earlier than in the district which has hitherto enjoyed a monopoly of supplying eastern cities. This is possible because the crop season along the Gulf Coast of Texas begins early and stays late. During one of these long periods two and three crops of many varieties of farm and garden products may be grown, and the soil apparently still be as vigorous as ever. Corn, oats, sorghum, hay, Irish potatoes, sweet potatoes, sugar cane, Egyptian and Sea Island cotton, Cuban tobacco, figs, pears, plums, grapes—the list might be expanded into a small catalogue. They all do well in this home of things that grow. The farmer and horticulturist does not have to urge forward his restless team of sun and soil. Rather they require holding back, lest the land produce too abundantly, beyond the capacity of its owner to properly care for the resultant crops.

Fish abound in all the streams, while in the waters of the Gulf they are so plentiful as to fill the local markets with a variety of finny creatures whose puzzling names sound queerly to the landsman. And oysters—they can be had for the mere trouble of gathering, if one will go to the Gulf.

The man who deliberately stays hungry and poor

in the Coast Country is worthless and lazy beyond redemption.

Lay siege to a South Texas plantation and you could not starve out the owner. He would still contentedly fill his old cob pipe with home grown tobacco, every bit as good as the imported leaf; and shake down ripe walnuts and pecans from trees in the timber lot for winter use. Luscious pears, peaches, strawberries and figs would form his dessert ten months in the year. Hardly a day would pass without fresh vegetables on the table plucked from his own truck patch. From the product of white acres of cotton and flocks of sheep could be fashioned homespun garments good enough for anybody.

ONLY TWO YEARS FROM THE SOD

Rich cane fields would contribute syrup and sugar. Fat hogs and sleek cattle would grow fatter and sleeker on river bottom corn and be transformed into bacon or beef. There is also plenty of fuel close at hand—while bayou and stream sustain fish in abundance. Even the vagrant winds bring in wild fowl from the Gulf. No one can be quite so independent as the man who owns a good farm in the Coast Country.

Cost of Land
Farm and garden land in the Gulf Coast belt now costs from $10 to $25 per acre in small tracts, with a reduction if bought in large bodies. In the immediate

vicinity of railroad depots and in some otherwise specially favored localities, a higher price is asked. There is considerable good fruit, berry and vegetable land, not yet taken, which can be purchased at an average price per acre of $10 to $15. Water rights for surface irrigation (as in California) are not necessary, because the abundant rainfall is supplemented by sub-irrigation.

Fine Markets

What do people do here? Galveston and Houston together comprise a population of 115,000 people. Galveston is the chief seaport of the Texas Coast, and Houston is its main railroad center. There is considerable manufacturing and the carrying trade employs large numbers of people. These persons and the truck farmers, fruit-growers and stock-raisers of the rural districts have a constant, near-by market, with thickly settled central and northern Texas not far away. The counties of Brazoria, Harris and Galveston are building a system of fine graded roads, part of them shelled, leading to neighboring trade centers. This employs some surplus labor and gives quick and easy access to local markets, while the splendid harbor facilities at Galveston afford the grower of grains and the producer of fruits a seaboard market for his surplus, at seaboard prices, untaxed by railway tolls.

Good Society

Good schools and churches are located in most of the settlements, some of them levying special tax for the support of their educational institutions. Newcomers need not fear they will lose sight of the little red school-house in the lane. The inhabitants are industrious and law-abiding, and the country is exempt from social disorders of all kinds. It is a good place to come with your family and settle.

Is There Room?

You need not fear that fruit culture or general farming is in danger of being overdone for many years. At Algoa, Alvin, Arcadia, Alta Loma, Hitchcock, Manvel, Pearland, Dickinson, North Galveston, La Porte, Clear Creek, Webster and Fairwood there are about 25,000 acres under cultivation. It would hardly make a good-sized cattle ranch up in north Texas.

The Future Elsewhere are given in detail the advantages of the flourishing towns that line the Santa Fe right-of-way from Hitchcock to Houston. Suffice to say, that the possessor of a ten or twenty-acre patch of ground in this region confidently believes he has title deeds to the best bit of real estate in the world; and what is more to the point, has figures to prove it.

Everybody in Texas "pulls" for Texas. Confidence begets confidence. It is the firm belief of every farmer on the Gulf, Colorado & Santa Fe Railway that he either has or will have an orchard just as good and just as paying as the finest one growing, and it does not require a very vivid stretch of the imagination to see, within a decade, an unbroken line of manorial gardens, country gentlemen's residences and closely cultivated farms all the way from Virginia Point to Houston.

FAMILY PETS

Gulf Coast Climate

• • •

The temperature along the Gulf Coast of Texas,
winter and summer, rarely varies to exceed 15° daily.
January is the coldest month in the year; during
twenty years the minimum temperature has fallen
below 20° in five years only, below 25° in ten years,
and below 30° in thirteen years. The temperature
along the immediate coast has not reached a maximum of 100° in this period, the highest record being
98° in August, 1874. July is the warmest month.
Killing frosts do not usually occur at Houston or
Galveston until after December 1 and the unwel-
come visitation is frequently delayed until January.
Four years in twenty there was no frost whatever at
Galveston, and in five different years there was but
a single frost. The last hard frost appears any time
between January 5 and February 1.

Two Decades Dr. I. M. Cline occupies the
position of local forecast offi-
cial, U. S. Weather Bureau, Galveston. He keeps a
careful tab on the daily weather and is authority on
the climate of Galveston. As Galveston may fairly
be considered representative of the Coast country,
his reports from a record of twenty years are of
great interest and value.

Dr. Cline publishes the following statistics with
regard to temperature : Normal, 52.3° in January
to 84.6° in July; highest monthly mean, 63.7° in
February to 86.2° in July; lowest monthly mean,
46.7° in January to 82° in July; maximum (highest)
75° in February to 98° in August; minimum (lowest)
11° in January to 70° in August; greatest monthly
range, 26° in February to 58° in January; least
monthly range 14° in August to 30° in November.
The normal precipitation is 52.48 inches yearly,
well distributed through the growing season; average
number of clear days per year, 133; average number
of partly cloudy days, per year, 140; average number of cloudy days per year, 92; average number of
days with some sunshine, 318. Prevailing direction
of wind is southeast; average hourly velocity ranges
from 8.0 miles in July to 11.9 in January.

Gulf Breezes The Texas coast winter is more a name than a fact. In summer the weather is without noticeable variation. This evenness of temperature is what makes it possible for the farmer to work comfortably out of doors nearly every day in the year. The genial southern trade wind, blowing over a thousand miles of salt water, brings both warmth and coolness, and contributes to maintain a similarity of seasons. This wind is always in motion, but rarely with enough violence to stir the dust. During a long period, only a few times has it blown a gale, while cyclones are unknown.

No matter how fervent may be the direct rays of the sun, a step into the shade brings pleasant relief. The nights are uniformly agreeable. Occasionally there is a hard frost, preceded by a strong wind from the north. It is the " norther," the fag end of which drops down from snow-covered Dakota prairies to inform Texans that Christmas is coming. Sensitive ears and tender plants have hardly felt the nip when the flurry is over, and the all-pervading Gulf breeze resumes its sway.

Expert's Views Hon. N. W. McLain, ex-director of the Minnesota state agricultural experiment station, is an enthusiastic convert to the allurements of the Gulf coast climate. In a newspaper article he says :

" Many of those who have lived there for years, speak confidently concerning the general healthfulness of this region, daily visited by the salt sea air. The trade-winds blow every day from the Gulf. They dispense life to vegetation and health to the inhabitants, wherever they reach. The long summers characteristic of this latitude, are by them rendered not only endurable but enjoyable.

" On Christmas Eve it seemed strange to see barefooted boys gazing at Santa Claus and his reindeer flying over artificial snow in the shop windows in Houston; and the salutation, ' Merry Christmas' sounded like a joke at a funeral. On New Years day, it seemed rather unseasonable to sit without a coat or hat, on a porch literally covered with roses, and elegant Marechal Niels blooming out on the lawn. On the twelfth of January I pulled oranges from fine old trees, among the most luxuriant gardens and lawns in Victoria. The nineteenth day of

18

January I walked through a small field of alfalfa sown the twenty-eight day of last October. The growth completely covered the ground, and the plants averaged eighteen inches in height. January 22d, in the gardens and fields near Alvin, I found the people picking strawberries."

No Malaria

Malaria is not prevalent in the country except when invited by carelessness or ignorance. Though this is a flat region, it has but few tracts of swampy land of small extent. Where forests occur, along the bayous, they are devoid of undergrowth; a sign that nothing is present productive of ague. The surplus rainfall drains into the Gulf—chills and fever only appearing sporadically along overflowed and undrained river bottoms. On the high open prairies, malaria is an almost unknown visitor, except where water is permitted to remain stagnant.

Colds and catarrh cause more suffering and deaths in the New England states alone, than the combined diseases of the Gulf Coast. No deadly epidemic diseases have visited this section for a quarter of a century. Periodical fevers are almost entirely absent.

Houston

Galveston and Houston are both healthful cities. Dr. Robt. McElroy, city health officer at Houston, says:

"The health of the city of Houston compares favorably with any city in the United States. Our death rate for the three past years was as follows: 1895, 13.5 per 1,000; 1896, 10.4; 1897, 13.5. Malaria, which was prevalent here in the early days, is comparatively unknown now, due principally to our fine quality of artesian water, of which there is an inexhaustible supply. More sewerage and better surface drainage also adds much to our improved condition. Contagious diseases are comparatively unknown. Our mild and even temperature, our supply of good water, together with our Gulf breeze, makes Houston one of the most desirable places to live in found anywhere in the South."

Galveston

From a recent report issued by Dr. W. C. Fisher, health officer, Galveston, it is learned that the general health of that city has been good, notwithstanding the outbreak of dengue fever during the fall of 1897. Statistics show that out of a population of 50,000 there were only 166 deaths during the months of August, September and October, 1897, as against 175 in 1896 and 187 in 1895. This too with a growing population. Increased sanitary efficiency has brought about this condition of affairs. When the $300,000 appropriated for municipal sewerage has been spent, the general healthfulness of Galveston will be even better. During 1897 the death rate per thousand was a fraction under 14, which is a good showing. It is noteworthy that typhoid fever, diphtheria, scarlet fever, cholera infantum, and other like diseases, are almost unknown here. For example, there were only twenty deaths from typhoid, scarlet, malarial and continued fever; and but eight from diphtheria in that year.

HOTEL AT GALVESTON BEACH.

finally The summers in Texas come early and stay late. If that long succession of warm and sunshiny days when one instinctively seeks the shady side of the street becomes monotonous to those who cannot get away for a summer vacation, there is, to offset this, only two months of winter, and that resembles a northern October. You will like it here when once acquainted. There is a fascination in what at first sight appears undesirable. The soothing Gulf airs are a perpetual invitation to cease worry and fret and hurry. They call to just enough indolence to prevent the human machine from too hastily wearing out. It is not a misdemeanor to be a trifle lazy in Texas.

Towns and Colonies

• • •

Below may be found a detailed description of the more important cities, towns and colonies situated on or contiguous to the Gulf, Colorado & Santa Fe Railway in the Gulf Coast country. The various Mennonite colonies are mentioned elsewhere.

Algoa The town of Algoa and its fruit land suburbs lies on the main line of the Gulf, Colorado & Santa Fe Railway, midway between Houston and Galveston. The location is a favorable one, both as regards quality of soil and nearness to important markets. The town proper is growing nicely, but no effort has been made to boom it—rather it has been the desire to first settle up the fertile surrounding country. A first-class shelled road leads from Algoa over a free wagon bridge to Galveston, so that products can be rapidly handled either by rail or wagon.

Some 2,000 acres of land adjoining Algoa have been platted into small tracts, ranging in size from two to forty acres. Each tract fronts on a public road and all are within one and a quarter miles of the station. The object has been to make this an ideal place for orchards, gardens, etc. There will be no taxes to pay here until the year 1900. Prices of land are governed by location; liberal terms offered actual settlers.

Alta Loma Alta Loma (population 700) is the first station beyond Hitchcock, being seventeen miles from Galveston, on the main Gulf, Colorado & Santa Fe line. It is the center of the Gulf Coast's magnificent fruit belt — a high prairie, heavily sodded with native grasses, and draining to the Gulf by an almost imperceptible descent.

The soil is a black sandy loam, several feet thick, with a yellowish clay subsoil, all underlaid with coarse gravel.

Alta Loma has plenty of pure fresh water, obtained from artesian wells at a depth of 550 to 700 feet. In this vicinity are nineteen artesian wells. The water works for the city of Galveston were

RESIDENCES AT ALTA LOMA AND ALVIN.

located here at a cost of about a million dollars. Five million gallons of water are delivered in the city every twenty-four hours.

The entire tract of 8,000 acres is surveyed into subdivisions of ten, twenty and forty acres, and is traversed by roads so arranged as to afford every ten-acre parcel easy access to the station.

Alta Loma has a fine public school building with an attendance of 150 children; has two churches, Baptist and Presbyterian; has a first-class canning factory and preserving works, the plant representing an outlay of more than $10,000 and doing a prosperous business; also has a shirt and overall factory employing quite a number of operatives. The township has about thirty miles of graded roads and a fine system of drainage. Hundreds of acres are now planted in fruit trees, vegetables and flower gardens. "Alta Loma," in the language of its founder, "has not a man, woman or child but what is well clothed and well fed. Its people are healthy, prosperous, law-abiding and happy."

Alvin In Brazoria County, near Mustang Bayou, surrounded by fertile prairies, and at the junction of the Gulf, Colorado & Santa Fe main line and Houston branch, is the wide-awake city of Alvin. Its present population is estimated at 1,500 people, chiefly acquired within the past six years. There are about 4,000 people within three and a half miles of the center of town. All kinds of retail business are fully represented. Alvin now has several spacious school buildings,

A DOORYARD AT ALVIN.

several attractive church edifices and no saloons. Ice factory plants, two cotton gins and a vinegar establishment are recent acquisitions. There is an abundance of pure, palatable water, obtainable at a depth of 15 to 20 feet, and several strong flowing wells of choice artesian water.

The climate of this nook is even and healthy,

being pleasantly affected, summer and winter, by the Gulf breezes. The soil is a dark, sandy loam, with clay sub-soil, underlaid at a depth of 10 or 15 feet with water-bearing quicksand. Average annual rainfall is 45 inches.

The LeConte and Keifer pears here find a congenial home. Peaches, apricots and plums are successfully grown, and the Japan orange is being introduced. Grapes are a success, the dreaded grape rot being practically unknown. Strawberries do well, if the ground is properly prepared, the fruit ripening in January and continuing to yield until June. It is not uncommon to pick ripe strawberries here Christmas day. The cape jessamine is extensively cultivated around Alvin, forming an important product. All kinds of vegetables flourish—in fact, the briny atmosphere, sandy soil and early seasons make this the truck farmers' gold mine, two or three crops a year being easily grown. Three crops of Irish potatoes are frequently raised in one season. Dairy products command good prices, and poultry-raising is a source of profit.

The nearness of Houston and Galveston, with ample service over the Santa Fe Route, supplemented by excellent country roads, brings Alvin in close touch with unexcelled local markets. In March, April and May, 1897, the shipments by express from Alvin to northern and eastern markets amounted to 13,970 crates of strawberries. It is estimated that the daily income this season from strawberries will average $1,000 per day for the two shipping months.

Amsterdam

Amsterdam is a new town located about twelve miles south of Alvin, in the southeastern part of Brazoria County. This town was started about two years ago by the Texas Colonization Co., which company owns an adjoining tract of 50,000 acres.

The land is bounded on the east by Chocolate Bayou and on the west and south by Bastrop Bayou and Bastrop Bay. The soil is mostly a heavy black, with considerable black-sandy loam; it is well-drained and very productive. A great many tracts have already been sold to actual settlers, who have built very comfortable homes.

Chocolate Bayou is navigable several miles above this property and boats make regular trips.

This is an exceptional body of land, owing to

proximity to the Gulf and excellent drainage as well as the superior quality of the soil. Prices range from $12.50 to $15 per acre, on very favorable terms to actual settlers. The way to get to this property is to buy a ticket over the Santa Fe Route and get off at Alvin, taking a private conveyance thence to Amsterdam.

Arcadia Arcadia was settled in the spring of 1890. It is situated on the line of the Gulf, Colorado & Santa Fe Railway, twenty-one miles from Galveston, and twenty-nine feet above sea level. The soil is divided into a sandy and black loam, underlaid with yellow clay at an average depth of one foot. For vegetables the sandy loam is generally preferred, though both are good for fruits.

The whole country is sub-irrigated at a depth of five or six feet, rendering it drouth proof so far as trees are concerned, although even vegetables rarely suffer.

Artesian water can be had at a depth of 100 to 600 feet, the quality being better at the greater depths. Every variety of vegetable succeeds well. Tomatoes ripen by the middle of May; strawberries are ready for picking last of February, and bear abundantly until June, a yield of $150 to $300 per acre not being uncommon. LeConte and Keifer pears are always vigorous, absolutely healthy, and bear an average of eight bushels to each tree six years old. American grapes are uniformly healthy, productive and free from rot or mildew. Cotton does well without manuring, the yield ranging from one-half to a full bale, and in lower locations sugarcane is a success; it is not hurt by frost before the first of December and rarely prior to the middle of January. Pears have been planted here on 3,000 acres and peaches on 200 acres. The largest orchards are owned by B. F. Johnson, C. Peterson, J. Wharton Terry, C. E. Angell and E. C. Lamb.

Whether the weather is wet or dry, there is no malaria, the sea breeze sweeping it away. Land is for sale at reasonable prices.

Arcola Arcola, in Fort Bend County, is the pretty name of a pretty town on the Gulf, Colorado & Santa Fe Railway, where that road connects with the International & Great Northern and the Sugarland & Arcola Railways. This promising place is eighteen miles from Houston and forty-three miles from Galveston.

DECEMBER VIEW OF A HOME IN ARCADIA.

The country roundabout is filling up with a desirable class of farmers, one hundred families having settled here, and the land has proven to be the equal of any along the Gulf Coast. Here is the dividing line between the immense stretch of black prairie extending eastward to Galveston Bay and the bottom lands of Oyster Creek and Brazos River on the west. West of Arcola the bottom lands have been utilized as cotton, sugar and corn plantations; they are now being divided into farm tracts and rapidly taken up by small farmers. The eastern prairies were originally devoted to the grazing of cattle; these also are being placed upon the market in small holdings.

Good drinking and stock water is obtained anywhere in the Arcola region at a depth of 20 to 40 feet. Pure artesian water flows freely when tapped 300 to 800 feet below the surface.

Nearly everything grows here. Cotton makes one bale to the acre; the corn product is 40 to 50 bushels per acre; oats are a success, the annual yield per acre averaging 60 to 75 bushels.

At Arcola is located the sugar plantation and factory of J. H. B. House. Cane yields 20 to 30 tons per acre and the factories pay about $3 per ton for it.

Truck gardening is also quite remunerative. Beans, onions, peas, cabbage, potatoes, beets, tomatoes, melons, etc., grow to perfection and bring high prices in adjacent markets. From $200 to $500 can be made from a winter garden of two acres, and the same ground planted in summer with grains. Pears, strawberries and all kinds of fruit do well. Tame grasses—timothy, crimson clover, bermuda and alfalfa—are successfully grown.

Arcola has three railroads, low freight rates, two sugar factories, a lumber yard, two hotels and livery stable. The town desires a general store, cotton gin, newspapers, brickyard, drug store, canning factory and floral garden.

Edna Edna, Jackson County (population 2,000) lies near the waters of Matagorda Bay, but has little water front, thus being beyond the range of any coast storms. The land is level. Much of it needs artificial drainage to become productive; this can easily be accomplished by taking advantage of the many fresh water creeks, such as Mustang, Sandy, Navidad, Lavaca, Arenosa, Benan,

Coxe's and Keller. These streams are skirted with timber, furnishing an abundance of fuel and fence posts. About 70 per cent. is prairie and 30 per cent. timber.

The soil is fertile, producing corn, cotton, vegetables and fruits; corn yields an average per acre of 30 bushels; sweet potatoes, 200 bushels, prairie hay, one ton, and cotton 300 pounds. With proper cultivation pears are particularly successful. Good water is plentiful. The climate is healthful.

Edna, the county seat, is located on the line of the Southern Pacific Co. sixty-seven miles west of Rosenberg. It is a growing town of 1,500 inhabitants, closely in touch with the surrounding country. Edna's public schools, churches and stores are far above the average.

Unimproved lands, in tracts of almost any size, may be bought at $4 to $10 per acre. Higher prices are charged for lands near the county seat and railroad, or for improved farms. Prospective settlers in the Coast Region of Texas are invited to examine what is offered in the vicinity of Edna, in case they should not find exactly what is wanted at a point nearer the Gulf, Colorado & Santa Fe Railway.

El Campo

Six years ago there was no El Campo. Today the town has a population of over 1,000. More than twenty new business enterprises have been established here within the past six months. If you ask what makes the place grow, it may be stated as one reason that Wharton County is being rapidly populated by a very enterprising class of people, largely consisting of Swedes. There are very few negroes.

Around El Campo is some of the richest soil in Texas, high and comparatively dry. The surrounding country, which was once a large cattle pasture, is being divided into fruit and cotton farms.

El Campo has butchers, bakers, lumbermen, bankers, grocers—in fact every leading branch of trade is represented. The New York, Texas & Mexican Railway furnishes good shipping facilities.

The business district is composed of substantial wooden structures of modern architecture, while large, spacious churches have been erected by several denominations.

Fairbanks Fairbanks is located twelve miles northwest of Houston, on the Houston & Texas Central Railroad and on the main county thoroughfare, called the Washington County Road. This is now being macadamized; several miles are already completed, and work is rapidly progressing on about five miles more, taking the road to within two and one-half miles of Fairbanks.

The land in that vicinity is a black, sandy loam, mostly prairie, with strips of timber along the creeks. The elevation is from five to eight feet to the mile, which affords excellent natural drainage in connection with the railroad and county road ditches running through the center of the property, and a creek on either side.

The lands around the town are being rapidly settled by thrifty northern farmers, who seem to be contented and doing well. The prices range from $5 to $10 per acre. There is a sawmill and planing mill within four miles of Fairbanks, which supplies cheap building material. The best of well water can be had at the depth of 15 to 30 feet at a cost of 50 cents per foot with pipe and pump all complete.

A school, postoffice, depot and express office are part of the conveniences of the town. Newcomers have organized and expect to raise vegetables and melons in quantities, so that they can ship in carload lots to northern markets. Some of the finest vegetables and melons on the Houston market in the past two years were raised at Fairbanks, and a number of carloads were shipped to northern markets with very satisfactory results.

Mr. C. W. Hahl has several acres of canaigre planted which is doing nicely, and promises to be a profitable crop; this is used for tanning purposes. It is becoming very popular where introduced and the demand cannot be supplied. The profit per acre, at a conservative estimate, will be from $40 to $50.

Galveston Great cities rise and flourish in response to a need. Rarely are they created by individual fiat or caprice.

Galveston supplies a distinct want, that of ocean port for the Southwest, and therefore will grow steadily year by year, keeping pace with the territory it serves. The city is built on the extreme eastern end of Galveston Island, just off the Gulf Coast of Texas,

THE EASTERN SECTION OF GALVESTON.

is six miles in area, and has a population of nearly 60,000. .

This fact appears remarkable; that a city of that size should transact business equal to other communities with three or four times more inhabitants. The anomaly is easily explained. The finest landlocked harbor on the Gulf of Mexico has given Galveston an immense carrying trade. Here come ships from European and South American ports to carry away our cotton, corn and wheat, in exchange for money or foreign commodities. So profitable has been the handling of these exchanges that conservative merchants and brokers were content to reap assured gains without seeking to bring in strangers by heralding to the outside world the city's manifest advantages. Already this is the third richest city in the United States according to population.

Galveston was not discovered in the true sense of the word, until a few years ago. Then the great West awoke to the fact that by means of the Santa Fe Route it was linked to a first-class deep water port, the largest and deepest on the Gulf Coast, several hundred miles nearer the interior than is New York City. For example: Galveston is 220 miles nearer to St. Louis, 730 miles nearer Denver and 483 miles nearer Kansas City than New York is.

The United States Government estimates that $6,200,000 is required to secure a channel of sufficient depth across the bar at the entrance of the bay. Now there is nearly 27 feet of water at average tides, which will be increased to accommodate any craft that floats. Jetty construction was begun in 1885, but work was not actually pushed until 1890. The south jetty is seven and one-half miles long and the north arm has been extended nearly six miles.

During 1896 there arrived at Galveston 28 vessels from foreign ports, of which number one-sixth carried cargoes, not including the small local craft. The clearances were 303, all with cargoes. The number of vessels entered in the coastwise business that year was 369. A gratifying increase in ocean trade is reported for 1897. As an exporting city Galveston ranks fifth, and has regular steamer lines to Houston, Key West, New York, Brazos, Santiago and Morgan City; also between Galveston and the foreign ports of Hamburg, Bremen, Liverpool, Manchester, Tampico and Vera Cruz.

Four miles of completed wharves, on the bay

31

front, with room for more, amply accommodate
existing traffic. Four immense grain elevators have
been erected, with storage capacity of 2,500,000
bushels; other elevators are projected. During the
commercial season, after September 1, the docks are
filled with bales of cotton. Cotton is the chief staple
of Texas and half of it comes to Galveston, making
this the second cotton port of America. Every bale
of cotton leaves in the city from $1 to $1.50 to pay
for handling, wharfage, etc.

Cotton and woolen mills, bagging, binding, twine,
rope and lace factories are established here; the total
of manufacturing establishments is 43. The fish
and oyster business will soon rival that of Baltimore.

The total exports for 1896 amounted to $56,000,-
000; customs-house receipts for 1896, $191,945.

COTTON WHARF, GALVESTON.

These figures give a fair idea of the business passing through Galveston.

Another factor of Galveston's prosperity is its
selection as headquarters for general offices and
shops of the Santa Fe System in Texas. Handsome
and substantial business blocks compactly line several wide streets, and merchants appear to be pros-
pering. The many beautiful homes, fine churches,
and numerous schools of Galveston attest its superior advantages as a residence city. Several large
hotels invite and foster transient custom. Many
residents of the interior Texas towns spend their
summers in this delightful spot, invigorated by the
cool sea breeze; and in the winter invalids and

pleasure seekers drop down from the North to enjoy May weather in December.

To miss seeing Galveston is not to have seen a representative Texas city.

Hitchcock Hitchcock, in Galveston County, on main line of Gulf, Colorado & Santa Fe Railway, fourteen miles from Galveston, is the original home of the pear industry in Texas. Here lived the eminent horticulturist, H. M. Stringfellow, who first discovered that this section could produce with profit the finest pears in the world. The attractive home, beautiful grounds and well-kept orchards formerly belonging to him attest the admirable qualities of this place. The original Stringfellow orchard now includes probably the largest nursery in Texas; its beauty attracts many visitors.

Numerous strawberry patches and truck farms lie within a radius of three miles. The land is sub-irrigated. Good well water is found at a depth of twelve to eighteen feet, and there are thirteen flowing artesian wells, varying in depth from 400 to 700 feet, with a flow ranging from 45 to 145 gallons per minute—the water rising twenty-five and thirty-five feet above ground.

Several large rose nurseries are located here. Judge Austin owns a fine nursery, containing 30,000 roses and 1,000 magnolias. W. L. Schumate and Capt. J. Aiken have 250,000 rose bushes, and F. Renaud 30,000. Tourists can obtain, in season, beautiful bouquets of rosebuds to take north, if orders are placed a day ahead. Cape jessamines are a decided success at Hitchcock, and the Satsuma variety of Japan orange is quite popular.

Over 1,000 acres of the country immediately tributary to Hitchcock are planted with pear trees, 100 acres with strawberries, 100 acres with grapes and 500 acres are devoted to cultivation of other fruits and vegetables. H. N. Lowrey, three miles west of Hitchcock, has planted 10,000 pear trees, 3,000 peach trees and 4,000 plum trees. The Wheeler Fruit Company has 11,000 pear trees and 25 acres in strawberries.

Persons desiring to invest in small fruit farms will do well to visit Hitchcock. At this point and Alvin enough has been accomplished to prove beyond cavil, that the coast country of Texas cannot be surpassed for productiveness.

33

LIGHT GUARDS ARMORY.   GOVERNMENT BUILDING AND POST OFFICE.   RESIDENCE OF S. K. DICK.

Houston If steamships made Galveston, railroads have made Houston—that prosperous and beautiful city of over 65,000 people which has grown up at the head of tide-water navigation, fifty-five miles from the head of the jetties at Bolivar Peninsula. A proposition is before Congress to deepen and widen the channel connecting Houston with the Gulf, thus increasing its shipping facilities. The proposed dimensions of this channel are 25 feet deep and 100 feet wide. When completed this will materially add to Houston's already great commercial importance.

PRESBYTERIAN CHURCH, HOUSTON.

The city was founded in 1821 and has grown from 29,000 inhabitants in 1890 to its present size. Nearby are immense forests of pine, oak, etc., and the profusion of magnolia groves in the suburbs has given it the name of the "Magnolia City."

These are some of the things that Houston offers the newcomer:

A healthful and enjoyable semi-tropical climate; mean summer temperature of 90° and average winter temperature of 60°; sweet, pure and soft artesian water; a low death rate—only nine to the thousand; ·

fifty miles of paved streets—vitrified brick, stone
and wood; no stagnant water, and an admirable sewerage system; handsome public and business buildings, and many beautiful private residences; the finest electric street railway system in the South, 35
miles completed; a taxable valuation of $22,000,000,
the rate being $2 per $100; a high school and 15
public schools for benefit of 10,000 children.

The bank clearances were over $231,000,000 for
fiscal year ending July 1, 1897. Three million dollars are invested in building associations, $350,000
in transportation lines, and $4,600,000 in manufac-
turing and industrial establishments, including six
cotton compresses and four cotton seed oil mills.
There is plenty of money here to do business with.

BUSINESS BLOCK AT HOUSTON.

Eleven trunk lines of railroad enter Houston,
affording ample means for traffic with half of the
vast area between the lower Mississippi River and
the Pacific. The roads actually centering in this
city have a mileage of 5,817 and the connecting sys-
tems a mileage of 31,000. Seven of them have their
general offices and shops here, disbursing $400,000
annually, and the Santa Fe is erecting a handsome
new passenger depot to accommodate its increasing
traffic. The jobbing houses of Houston do an immense business ($32,000,000 annually) among the tim-
ber regions of East Texas, the central cotton section

of the State, and the sugar districts of Texas and southwestern Louisiana. Eighty miles of switches, side-tracks, etc., afford complete facilities for handling freight. In addition to the facilities offered by the Santa Fe Route for rail transportation to seaboard, a system of barges deliver cargoes on board ocean steamers at Galveston without trans-shipment.

Other items of interest are the gas works, with a plant capacity for 100,000 population; public school buildings valued at $365,000, and fine artesian water, the average supply being 3,000,000 gallons, drawn from 30 wells.

As a cotton market. Houston takes a front rank. The gross receipts for season of 1897-98 were 1,161,133 bales. The annual lumber trade amounts to over $25,000,000.

The principal trade of the city of Houston is in Texas products, such as cotton, sugar, molasses, rice, fruits, lumber, wool and hides. Houston has an enviable future before it, if the growth of the last decade should be continued. Its location is such as to command a large share of the industrial prosperity of Southern Texas, and it will always be an important factor in that region. Every home-seeker should visit Houston.

Acknowledgement is hereby made of the courtesy of Dr. V. S. MacNider and Messrs. Blackburn & Bailey, in furnishing photos of Houston for reproduction herein.

La Porte The confluence of Buffalo Bayou and San Jacinto River form what is known as San Jacinto Bay, a body of fresh water seven miles long by from one to two miles in width. At the lower end it is almost separated from Galveston Bay, the great inland sea of Texas, by a promontory which ranges in width from 1,500 feet at its point to one and one-half miles at its base. This promontory has an elevation of forty feet above San Jacinto Bay, and thirty-five feet above Galveston Bay, the former bank being abrupt, while the latter recedes in graceful, easy terraces almost to the water's edge. Beautiful hardwood trees, green ten months in the year, draped with Spanish moss and mistletoe, fringe the borders of the promontory, and picturesque little islands of the same timber give a most pleasing effect to the general landscape.

By water this promontory is located forty miles

from Houston and thirty miles from Galveston, but by rail or wagon road it is but twenty-four miles from Houston and thirty-two miles from Galveston, being practically, either by land or water, midway between the two great cities of Texas.

On this strip of land the town of La Porte is situated. It is already quite a place with ample railroad, navigation, telegraph and telephone facilities. La Porte possesses churches, school-houses, hotels, livery stables, stores of all varieties and well-equipped bathing houses. The surrounding agricultural country (and there is none better in the state) is well developed. The proposed great ship channel will make it an important commercial point.

La Porte is becoming widely known throughout Texas as a delightful summer resort. It is a veritable Coney Island for Houston, and summer excursions from that city are frequent. The hunting and fishing in the fall and winter attract many sportsmen from the North, who often remain for months. The bathing, boating, fishing and sailing facilities are unexcelled.

Surrounding La Porte, together with the adjoining tract of land known as South La Porte, is about 4,000 acres of land, which has been laid off in small tracts for fruit and vegetable farmers. The prices of town lots in La Porte and its neighboring farms are reasonable and the terms easy.

In addition to its properties at La Porte, the American Land Company (with headquarters at Chicago, St. Louis and Houston) also has charge of the tracts at Meadowbrook and Webster; correspondence invited.

Manvel The settlement of Manvel is situated in Brazoria County, on the Gulf, Colorado & Santa Fe Railway main line, midway between Arcola and Alvin, and is thirty-six miles distant from Houston. Two hundred heads of families have settled within a few miles of the depot. Many of them are Dunkards, a religious sect whose industry and thrift are proverbial.

It has been demonstrated that it is as fertile as any other portion of the coast. Nearly 4,000 acres of land has been cut up into ten, twenty and forty acre tracts, lying near the town site, the selling price being $15 to $30 per acre. The summer of 1897 the cultivated acreage was as follows: Pears and other fruits, 250 acres; strawberries, 100 acres; vegetables, 50 acres.

Cotton is being extensively planted and the region around Manvel bids fair to be as great a cotton and corn country as Northern Texas. The soil is of two kinds, black-sandy and black-waxy, the latter being well adapted for corn and cotton.

Five miles from Manvel is a choice tract of 20,000 acres, in a solid body, located on the west side of Chocolate Bayou. It has been surveyed, sub-divided and platted into lots of forty acres each, with road-ways for everyone, connecting with the main high-way, and so arranged that they can be conveniently cut into smaller lots of ten or twenty acres each.

Meadowbrook

Meadowbrook, Harris County, Texas, consists of about 20,000 acres of land, located in the celebrated South Texas Coast Country, and controlled by the American Land Co. It is within twenty miles of Houston, the county seat, which is the largest city of Texas.

The land is all a beautiful prairie, except that the banks of Buffalo Bayou and its tributaries are fringed with groves of hardwood timber, principally of the several varieties of oak, the utility of which for fuel, fence posts. etc., is apparent. Three railroads and three county roads pass through Meadowbrook, and it is perfectly drained by Buffalo Bayou, one of the important waterways of Texas, passing through the tract from the west to the east. Two railroad stations, with side-track and other shipping facilities, are already situated on Meadowbrook and arrangements are well under the way for the third.

This large body of land has been divided into farms of 160 acres each, and graded roads are being constructed along the section lines, at right angles to Buffalo Bayou, thus affording each quarter section the double purpose of an outlet to the railroads and county roads as well as drainage to the Bayou. The main road from Houston has been graded and grav-eled to within nine miles of Meadowbrook and will be completed in the near future.

Fruits of nearly every variety, both large and small, all kinds of vegetables, and the great staples of cot-ton, corn, oats, sugar and hay give the most grati-fying results at Meadowbrook. Improved farms surrounding this tract show positive evidence as to what can be produced and it has been placed on the market at prices and terms, that, together with its general conditions, invite comparison with any other lands in that most favored portion of these United States.

Pearland

The town of Pearland, fifteen miles south of Houston, on the Gulf, Colorado & Santa Fe Railway, is the center of a splendid country. The town-site has been laid off on a modern plan, with boulevards and broad streets, reserving locations for churches and parks. It is expected to build up here a model community. Pearland is surrounded by thousands of acres of the finest prairie land, nearly every acre of which is suited to fruit, vegetable and general farming. Ten thousand acres of the land immediately surrounding Pearland have been sub-divided into ten, twenty and forty-acre tracts, which are being sold at $15 to $25 per acre, one-third cash, the balance in one and two years. Each tract will front a broad, graded road.

Pearland is now a thriving village of 300 inhabitants. It has schools and churches and is surrounded by a desirable class of citizens who are engaged in fruit-raising and general farming. Considering age, Pearland can show one of the finest pear orchards along the coast.

Richmond

Richmond is the county seat of Fort Bend County. It is a prosperous and enterprising town, containing about 1,500 people. Its location on the west bank of the Brazos River, within a short distance of the Falls of the Brazos, will give it, when the 3,000 horse power there is fully developed, a commanding position as a manufacturing center.

Richmond is not only a pleasant place in which to live, but it is a good place to do business in. Already the town possesses water works, an electric light plant, bank, three railroads, a telephone exchange, two cotton gins and a grist mill. One notable feature is an immigrant house, where any person who has bought land in the county or who deposits a certain amount of money in bank is granted free house rent for a month or so in order to make ready for the occupancy of his new home.

Not content with being in the center of a magnificent agricultural country, Richmond is reaching out for various enterprises and affords excellent opportunities for the location of manufactories based on cotton, timber and sugar.

Rosenberg Rosenberg is very favorably situated in Fort Bend County, at the junction of the main lines of the Gulf, Colorado & Santa Fe Railway and Southern Pacific Co. It is also the northern terminus of the New York, Texas & Mexican Railway, and the Rosenberg, Damon Mound & Gulf Railroad. It lies 66 miles north of Galveston and 36 miles west of Houston; contains 750 inhabitants (mainly from northern states) and is the natural trade center of a rich country. This outlying territory consists of say 400 sections of high prairie lands and rich river bottoms where, without fertilizing, the average crops are forty bushels of corn, seventy bushels of oats, three tons of millet hay and one bale of cotton per acre. All kinds of fruits—except apples—are raised here, as well as all varieties of vegetables.

The Brazos River bottoms contain great forests of oak, ash and other hard woods, interspersed with magnificent plantations where corn, cotton and sugar cane grow luxuriantly. Desirable farming lands lying within a radius of three to eight miles from town command $8 to $25 per acre. Taxes are low, about $1 per hundred on a 40% valuation.

Rosenberg has several church societies and fine school buildings. Being 132 feet above sea level and 40 feet above the Brazos, good drainage and consequent good health is assured. Excellent water is obtainable at convenient depths.

Its location in the midst of forests of red and white cedar, cypress, ash, etc., makes Rosenberg a desirable place for the manufacture of woolen goods. A canning factory would also do well here. The transportation facilities above mentioned give this town manifest advantages as a distributing point. Persons desiring further information should address Geo. B. Lang, Secretary Progressive Association, Rosenberg, Texas.

Sealy The thriving town of Sealy is situated fifty miles west of Houston and ninety-five miles northwest of Galveston at the junction of the

41

Gulf, Colorado & Santa Fe Railway and the Missouri, Kansas & Texas Railroad, and has a population of about 1,500. It is the first division on the Santa Fe line out of Galveston, with a round-house and other necessary improvements.

The town is situated on a slight elevation above the surrounding country, just at the beginning of the rolling land adjacent to the coast country proper, thereby having excellent natural drainage and splendid water, and is one of the healthiest places in South Texas. The Brazos River is five miles distant. Sealy possesses a first-class public school system and churches of the various denominations.

The citizens liberally support a weekly newspaper, and the town boasts of a tannery, harness and saddle manufactory, a mattress factory, also two of the finest steam cotton gins in this part of the country, one of them having just lately been purchased to be put in operation this summer. A complete electric plant of 700 light capacity is building. A commodious opera house and public amusement hall, five first-class hotels, besides numerous business edifices, complete the list of principal buildings.

In addition to the magnificent resources of Austin County elsewhere briefly alluded to, it may be said that the excellent railroad facilities at Sealy make the raising of canteloupes and watermelons one of the leading industries of the region. About 500 acres of melons will be marketed at Sealy this year to be shipped north. The value of adjacent farming lands varies from $5 to $40 per acre.

Superior Lies thirty-three miles from Galveston, twenty miles from Houston, and begins just two miles north of Alvin, on the Houston branch of the Santa Fe, with eight daily passenger trains. This is a new town located upon a tract of 10,000 acres of land purchased by the Southern Homestead Company of Houston, and characterized as the finest large body of land along the Gulf Coast. It is in the center of the newly developed fruit and vegetable belt and is being highly improved with finely graded roads and ample ditches. Many settlers have located at this place.

Wallis The thrifty town of Wallis (population 500) is located in Austin County, at the junction of the San Antonio & Aransas Pass Railway with the Gulf, Colorado & Santa Fe Railway, eighty-two miles north of Galveston and forty-five miles west of Houston. Its twenty business houses carry large stocks of goods and it has a wide-awake newspaper. Educational and social advantages are as advanced as those of any like settlement in Southern Texas. Railroad facilities are unusually good.

Austin County is briefly described under another caption. A few additional facts pertaining especially to the territory surrounding Wallis will be of interest. The lands between the Brazos and San Bernard Rivers are of inexhaustible fertility, being as rich now as when first cultivated forty years ago. The prairie lands are worth $5 to $20 per acre; bottom lands, $10 to $30.

Cotton is a crop that never fails. In 1897 Wallis marketed 5,000 bales. In a good season the output is about 8,000 bales. Corn averages 40 to 60 bushels to the acre. Vegetables and small fruits are successfully raised. The country around Wallis is inhabited to a considerable extent by Germans, who with their customary industry have made valuable improvements. Homeseekers who prefer to get back from the Coast and at the same time have the benefit of the Gulf breezes, should investigate the claims of Wallis and vicinity.

Webster The colony of Webster, Harris County, Texas, is located on a tract of about 5,000 acres of land midway between Houston and Galveston, on the line of the Galveston, Houston & Henderson Railroad, over which also operates two other lines, thus practically affording it the advantages of three railroads. It has a depot, side-track and other ample shipping facilities. Population about 300.

This is a magnificent body of black prairie land, perfectly drained, and is in the midst of the great fruit and vegetable district of South Texas. Well developed farms in and surrounding Webster evidence its great productiveness. Clear Lake, a navigable stream and tributary of Galveston Bay, directly adjoins this land and its settlers have all the advantages of water competition. Real estate at Webster will be sold in tracts to suit the purchaser and at very reasonable prices and terms, considering the location. The American Land Company is developing this property.

45

Wharton Rosenberg station, on the Gulf, Colorado & Santa Fe Railway, is the most convenient point of departure for a large section of country to the southwest. After passing through Fort Bend County, the next one is Wharton, dubbed by its enthusiastic inhabitants the banner county of the coast country. It is in the second tier back from the Gulf. The county is watered by Peach, Jones, Sandies and Mustang creeks, also the Bernard and Colorado Rivers. Wharton contains 1,172 square miles, a princely domain of 718,000 acres, three-eighths woodland and five-eighths open country; surface is level, divided equally between prairie and woodland; soil is alluvial and adapted to almost everything that grows in the south. Along the Colorado River especially the soil is of great depth. On the water courses there is a sufficiency of timber for firewood. Railroad facilities are excellent, the county being traversed by three lines. The average annual yield in Wharton County is 20,000 bales of cotton, 200,000 bushels of corn, 20,000 bushels of Irish potatoes, over 10,000 bushels of sweet potatoes, 20 cars of pecans, etc. Being in the fruit belt, everything of that kind does well here. Unimproved lands bring $5 to $15 per acre; improved, $15 to $30.

The town of Wharton, county seat, stands on the east bank of the Colorado River, 50 miles from the coast. It is the principal distributing point for Wharton and Matagorda counties. Present population, 2,000. Its business establishments have a heavy trade, and the social and educational advantages of the town have kept pace with its industrial growth.

Mennonite Colonies

• • •

The present exodus of Mennonites from various northern states to Southern Texas is in many respects a remarkable movement. Nothing like it has been witnessed for many years.

These Mennonites are a thrifty people, noted as home-builders. By hard work, prudence and foresight they have made a success of nearly all their undertakings. It seems to be their mission to be pioneers of farming industry.

They are an exceptional race. Piety and practical affairs go hand in hand While fearing God they do not fear Nature. No unfavorable combination of soil or climate or circumstances has ever routed them. They may leave one locality for another, but the migration is based on other grounds than failure at home. Each change is a step forward.

They are withal shrewd buyers, investigating carefully before pulling up stakes and starting anew. So well known is their sagacity in this respect that keen competition exists among holders of large bodies of raw lands whenever it is known that a new Mennonite enterprise is to be launched. It is a compliment to the resources of any country to be selected by the Mennonites for colonizing purposes, because by experience they have learned what good land is and will have no other.

Mr. W. B. Slosson, of Houston, Texas, who is at present the authorized general agent for the Mennonite colonies at Crosby, Ft. Bend, Thompson or Menno City, Westfield and Brookshire, was instrumental in bringing down to the Texas Gulf Coast more than a thousand Mennonites during the Fall of 1897. Nearly 400 have already located and many others are coming in from far away Oregon, South Dakota, Minnesota, Illinois and Iowa, as well as from Nebraska, Kansas, Oklahoma and Northern Texas. Mr. Slosson has acted in conjunction with a Committee of Eleven, many of them Mennonite preachers and all men of influence. The Santa Fe Route was unanimously chosen by them as the official line for transportation of settlers and goods, thereby further cementing a friendship which began when the Santa Fe brought the Mennonites over from Russia to America many years ago.

The question may be asked: Why are these people leaving their northern homes and coming so far south? An important reason is that the good cheap lands of the Middle West are almost gone and the tide of immigration must seek other outlets. One of these outlets is towards Southern Texas. For years the coast region was owned and controlled by cattle men; they did not want their great pastures cut up into small holdings. That day has passed, and they are inviting rather than repelling the advent of the farmer and fruit-raiser.

Another factor is found in the movement for deep-water harbors at Galveston and other points on the Texas coast, permitting the immense surplus crops of the northwest and southwest to be more easily and more profitably marketed than heretofore. This has widely advertised Southern Texas.

Other reasons, as detailed by the committee in their literature, may be briefly summed up in the items of a healthy climate, good water, excellent markets, no blizzards, sufficient rainfall, low taxes, cheap freight rates, cool Gulf breezes in summer, scarcely any winter, fruit culture successful, a diversity of crops possible, more than one crop a year obtainable in some instances, friendly neighbors, and an opportunity to build up a prosperous community of those holding the same faith and swayed by like traditions. Probably the three most important elements are cheap lands, large crops and a pleasant winter climate.

Brookshire A promising settlement has been started at Brookshire, thirty-five miles west of Houston, where good prairie lands may be obtained at prices varying from $5 to $8 an acre. About 6,500 acres have been secured. Hon. Fred. Harpster is in charge locally.

Crosby Colony Twenty-five miles north-east of Houston, in Harris and Liberty Counties, within seven miles of three railroad stations, is the flourishing colony of Crosby. The land is mainly a dark or black, sandy loam, rich, well-drained and well timbered. All the staple crops can be raised, as well as fruits and vegetables. Several streams afford an adequate water supply. This colony was organized with parties from Oregon, Kansas and South Dakota. The land is held at $5 to $8 per acre, and about 8,000 acres are available; 2214 acres already occupied.

A HILL OF STRAWBERRIES IN MARCH.

fort Bend The first colony located by the Mennonites was in Fort Bend County, seven miles south of Richmond and Rosenberg, on the Gulf, Colorado & Santa Fe Railway. Nearly 5,000 acres of black " hog-wallow " lands were bought for $10 per acre on favorable terms. More than forty families have already settled here and every week adds to their number. New houses have been built, the prairie broken, orchards planted, wells dug, and other improvements made. Schools, churches and store-buildings have been built and the success of the colony is assured.

Thompson or Menno City The second Mennonite Colony was placed at Thompson Station, eighteen miles northwest of Houston, in Harris County, on the Houston & Texas Central Railroad. About 3,000 acres of good black-sandy loam lands have been purchased, and over forty families already located. It is expected that a hundred additional families will follow soon. Several thousand acres more can be secured when needed. Prices range from $4.50 to $7.50 per acre. This is prairie land, with plenty of timber. Water is found at a depth of 15 to 30 feet. There is a fine road direct to the city of Houston. A saw mill and planing mill have been erected, and lumber can be obtained for $5 to $7 a thousand feet. This colony is locally known as Menno City, and the postoffice will soon be changed to correspond. Rev. H. A. Koehn, formerly of Newton, Kan., is the local agent at Menno City.

Westfield

The Westfield Colony was started by 115 persons who came in one party from Colorado. Members have since been received from several other states. The colony shows the effect of working together to a common end, for already extensive improvements have been made or are under way. Westfield is sixteen miles north of Houston, Harris County, on the International & Great Northern Railroad. A macadamized road connects the village with Houston. Several thousand acres of good black-sandy prairie land have been reserved, for sale at $5 to $6.50 per acre on terms to suit. Many of the old settlers in this locality are of German descent, having accumulated considerable of this world's goods. Schools and churches are within easy access. Rev. Henry Bergthold is the local agent.

HOUSTON HIGH SCHOOL.

Testimony of farmers

• • •

It is one thing to generalize; quite a different affair to state particular facts. One may fluently speak in an impersonal way and general terms of the glorious empire state of Texas. Such adjectives may mean much or little. To prepare a statement of what has been accomplished on your own tract of land, with conclusions drawn from personal experience, requires scientific accuracy. An imaginative discourse will not pass muster.

Bearing this in mind, and in order that the situation in Texas might be fairly presented to outsiders, we have asked several farmers and fruit-raisers to tell herein their own story of success or failure, for the guidance of others. What they say, follows:

Rev. henry Bergthold

Rev. Henry Bergthold, of Westfield, Texas, formerly of Colorado, is evidently well pleased with his Texas venture, as may be seen from the following letter recently written by him:

"I came here from Colorado, and was a member of the first committee sent out to locate Mennonite colonies. My report being favorable a large party of us left Colorado and settled here. I had been in several Western States looking for a location and felt the great responsibility in selecting a home for my family and friends. We are now in Harris County, Texas, 16 miles north of Houston, which is our market. Although having settled here only a few months ago, we are doing what we started out to do—getting homes. Lumber being cheap, we soon had our houses built. Now we are breaking prairie and planting our gardens and orchards.

"I never saw a country where people can live so cheaply as soon as they get started. We have German neighbors here who have got a better start in one year than they could in five years in Colorado.

"Not for a single moment have I ever regretted coming to this Coast Country, and it looks now as though we, and those of our people who are now coming to the Westfield colony, would all own lands and homes of our own in a short time."

TYPICAL SCENES ON A SOUTHERN PLANTATION.

Chas. Bushhausen Mr. Chas. Bushhausen lives at Pearland, Texas, within a mile of the station. He owns 41 acres of land, of which all but 10 are used in raising strawberries, cabbages, onions, beets, cotton and oats. Strawberries are his largest crop and cabbages the best paying one. His experience in fruit is limited to strawberries. Mr. Bushhausen considers them a paying crop, the best one for a small farm. He has experienced a partial failure with cotton.

The home market does not consume his entire product. For very early fruit and vegetables it pays to ship them a long distance. Medium early and late fruit and vegetables should be sold nearer home.

Mr. Bushhausen recommends the South Coast of Texas without any reservation whatever.

R. H. Bushway Mr. R. H. Bushway, of Alvin, Texas, contributes the following statement, under date of January 13, 1898:

"My native state is Illinois. I came to the Coast Country of Texas six years ago, since which time I have been continuously identified with the fruit industry. For the last four years my time has been devoted to the nursery business as founder and manager of the Alvin Nursery Co. Our grounds occupy forty acres of land, situated two and one-half miles from the city of Alvin. Ten acres of this land is in bearing pear orchard, ten acres in an orchard two years old, and twenty acres now being put into cultivation. Besides the above, we have fourteen acres under lease, mostly planted in strawberries and nursery stock. Aside from the nursery our only commercial crop is strawberries, which have proven extremely profitable when properly grown and marketed.

"The following statement taken from our books for 1896 shows results obtained:

```
Number of 24-quart crates shipped from 7 acres...512
Total receipts.....................................$1,217.00
Cost of 572 crates, at 18c.............$ 92.16
Cost of picking, at 60c. per crate ... 309.60
Nails, expenses, labor, etc..........  20.00    121.76
        Net proceeds of 7 acres...............$ 795.24
```

"Our berries are grown on black land without fertilizer of any kind, and by the system employed one man and team can plant and attend fifteen acres. By good cultivation and liberal application of commercial fertilizers, the above results can be increased threefold.

"In our six years' experience we have never had a crop failure, and only once a partial failure—even then good strawberry beds net their owners nearly $100 per acre. Such land as our berries are grown on can be bought in ten-acre blocks at from $15 to $30 per acre.

"While a large quantity of our products find a ready sale at good prices in the state, by far the greater percentage is shipped direct to the North, where the demand for our early berries and vegetables is only limited by our ability to produce. Almost our entire crop is shipped by express; however we hope by another year to see the acreage increased so that it will warrant a through freight service to such important points as Chicago, St. Louis and Kansas City, thereby reducing the cost of transportation to a minimum. We have been very successful in obtaining fancy prices for our early berries from northern markets and consider this outlet for our products practically unlimited, as we are fully three weeks earlier than our competitors.

"After six years of practical experience we have no hesitancy in affirming that every dollar intelligently invested in fruit growing in the Texas Coast Country will return three times the interest of the same amount invested in cotton or grain farming, proportionately to the capital put in.

"In regard to health will say that I came here badly affected with nasal catarrh and at the end of three years every symptom was gone, and nowhere does the general health appear so good.

"To the intelligent, industrious man or woman seeking to better their condition and acquire a home, the Texas Coast Country offers inducements not equalled by any other section—and to such is accorded a hearty welcome."

T. B. Davis Mr. T. B. Davis, of Arcola, came from Brazoria County, Mississippi, and bought 160 acres of prairie land two and one-half miles east of Arcola. Fifty-five acres are planted to cotton, corn, potatoes, berries, watermelons, vegetables and oats. Mr. Davis' best crop is cotton. He has had no experience with fruits. He is experimenting with a small orchard and believes pears and strawberries to be the leading fruits. He has never had a complete failure of any crop, although corn was cut short one season account dry weather.

He makes a fair profit every year and reports living expenses very moderate.

The school and church privileges at Arcola are good and taxes not too high.

The home market consumes all that can be raised, at a fair price. While having had no experience in shipping fruits or vegetables, Mr. Davis says the facilities for shipping are excellent. Furthermore he thinks that the climate is not excelled by any other country.

He recommends the Coast Country to men who have enough money on hand to pay for building and fencing; also sufficient means to carry them through one year with economy.

Franz Heinrichs

Mr. Heinrichs visited the Coast Country several times and assisted in locating the first three colonies. He is a representative Mennonite; has bought and is improving 310 acres of land in the Fort Bend Colony; prefers South Texas to Kansas, because he finds here copious rainfall, no blizzards, scarcely any winter, a healthy climate and pure water.

"I think it is a good place for poor people," writes Mr. Heinrichs, "as vegetables can be raised every month in the year and the cattle and sheep business pays well, with free range.

"A friend of mine who came here from South Dakota with weak lungs is now well. He could not walk a quarter of a mile up north, but took a stroll of three miles here with me last month.

"With good markets and low-priced land, close to deep water ports at Houston and Galveston, we are bound to make money. Our Mennonite people like this country and more are coming."

Jesse W. Hill

"I came to Texas from middle Tennessee," writes Mr. Jesse W. Hill, of Arcola, Tex. "My farm is situated two and one-half miles northeast of Arcola. It consists of 160 acres of black-sandy and black-waxy soil. The line of the Gulf, Colorado & Santa Fe Ry. is two miles away. Eighty-five acres are in cotton, corn, oats, potatoes and strawberries, with a little corn and peanuts. Cotton is the staple crop, although potatoes, oats and strawberries do well. I have three or four hundred fruit trees, all growing rapidly. Pears and peaches seem to be the leaders

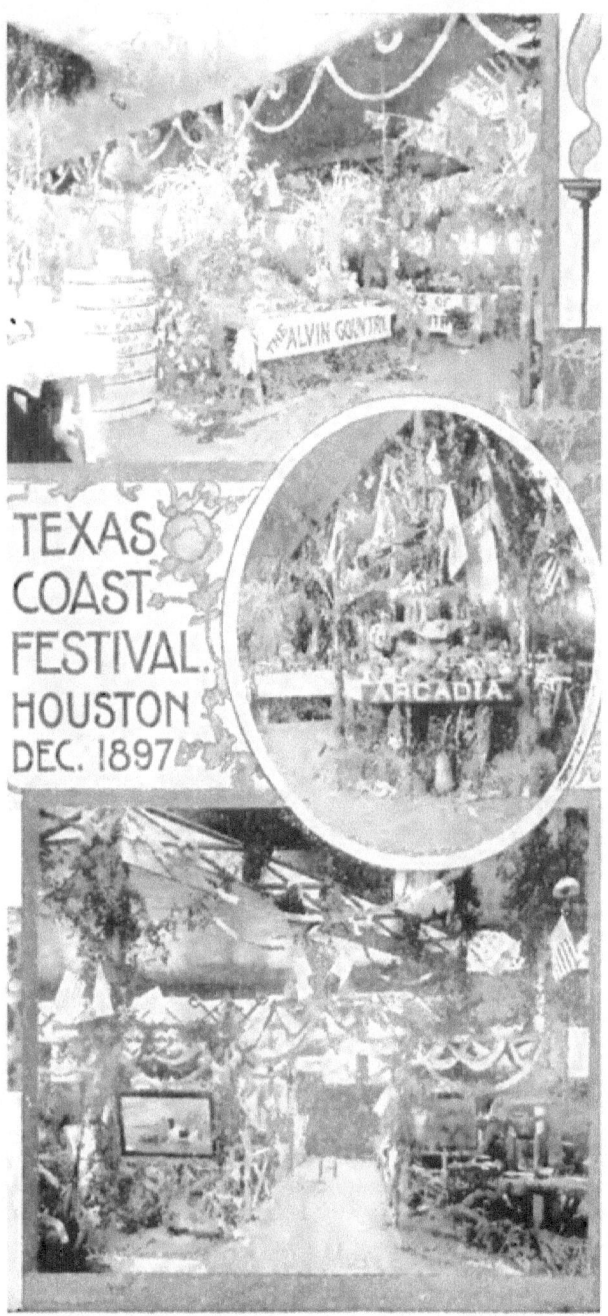

TEXAS COAST FESTIVAL ASSOCIATION, HOUSTON.

Had a partial failure once with corn, account drouth.

"By economy some profit can be realized. Markets are fairly good. I can sell everything I raise at living prices. Have not shipped any vegetables. The general health of the country is good. My family has had comparatively little sickness. Our health has been better here than for fifteen years past in other localities. Capacity for work is almost unlimited. I would recommend our country to any man who has enough means to improve his farm and pay expenses for a year. After that he can make a living all right."

B. F. Johnson Mr. B. F. Johnson, of Arcadia, Tex., is president of the Gulf Coast Horticultural Association, consisting of the counties of Brazoria, Galveston and Harris.

He came to the Lone Star State from Arkansas five years ago and owns sixty acres of land, three-fourths under cultivation. He reports that his best crop in quantity is Irish potatoes and that cabbages are the best in quality. Fruit trees are just coming into bearing. Has never had a partial or complete failure, except in the case of cotton. Lands that are in a good state of cultivation have paid a very nice income. Taxes are moderate. Schools very good, being supported wholly by the state school fund. Home market fairly good, in a small way; for large shipments other markets must be sought.

Mr. Johnson has shipped fruits and vegetables by both freight and express, and states that express rates do not leave a very large margin of profit. It is his idea that if the farmers combine their shipments into train loads they would make more money.

"I must say," writes Mr. Johnson, "I have never known of any section of country with such bright possibilities. I know we can grow as many Irish potatoes per acre as any section in the United States, and of as good a quality; besides we produce two crops instead of one."

Continuing: "The climate is as good as could be desired, and this region is simply superbly healthy. We have no need of doctors and away from the bayou there is no malaria. I have never known of a case of chills and fever. A neighbor, with nine in the family, has lived here five years and has never called a physician."

In conclusion Mr. Johnson recommends industrious settlers of small means to locate in his neighborhood, if they have sufficient "get up and get." Those who come expecting that dollars can be picked up off the prairie will be disappointed. There are only three things that grow in Texas without any effort on the part of the land owner, viz., prairie grass, cattle and mosquitoes, the latter for two or three weeks in the springtime only.

Jno. B. Klaassen

The following letter is from Mr. Jno. B. Klaassen, once a resident of Lehigh, Kansas, now living in Texas. He was one of the committee appointed by the Mennonites to locate their Texas colonies and has carefully inspected the Coast Country. Mr. Klaassen says:

" I was one of the Committee of Eleven that located the first three colonies in Texas and am sure I did the best work of my life in starting a movement of our Mennonite people in this direction. Several of our committee visited and inspected the Coast Country, and in September, 1897, we located the first three colonies.

" December 18, 1897, I brought my family and a car of goods over the Santa Fe Route to my 300-acre place in the Fort Bend Colony; this was thirty days ago, and already I have erected a house, two sheds and chicken-houses, have 160 acres fenced-in, two wells dug (30 feet deep each), 40 acres broken and am ready to put out an orchard and garden; will break this year 100 acres more.

" Horses, mules, young cattle and sheep all do well here, but it is not best to bring old cows. We have good health. My wife and children are pleased —no more drouths and blizzards for us.

" I am glad that this movement of our people to Texas is taking such a wide range, covering not only the northwestern states, but Oregon and Manitoba, and recent correspondence from Russia goes to show that it is becoming a matter of interest in other countries as well—but there is plenty of room in Texas and cheap lands; let them come."

Rev. H. A. Koehn

The following letter from Rev. H. A. Koehn, formerly of Kansas, now located at Menno City, Harris County, Texas, briefly gives his impressions of the Coast Country. Rev. Koehn is a prominent Mennonite preacher.

"I left Kansas and came here with this new colony because after careful investigation I found a much better climate, and because the lands here are much cheaper than in Kansas. I have now been located at the Menno Colony for several months; have built a house, and last week completed my barn, 20 x 32 feet, 14 feet high, with an L 14 x 20 feet, one story, shingle roof; material, pine lumber and cypress shingles; it cost me $61.45 for the whole barn. The lumber was hauled about ten miles from the mills.

"We have here a good settlement of Mennonites from the North, and every week adds to our numbers, yet there is plenty of room for others who wish to make homes of their own and are willing to work.

"There is good water and good health. We are much pleased with our new home. My wife and I brought with us ten children from Kansas. All are well, and under the good free schools of Texas, we will educate them here in both English and German.

"Most of our people have paid from $5 to $6 per acre for their land, and being near the largest city in Texas and on a railroad line, a bargain is secured. I hardly think good prairie lands can be bought elsewhere for so small a price as here. We all came over the Santa Fe road, and are much pleased with the treatment received by its representatives."

Eli Landreth Mr. Eli Landreth resides a quarter of a mile from Pearland station. He came to Texas from Iowa two years ago. His farm is a large one, consisting of 260 acres. Ninety acres are in cultivation, the main crops being oats, cotton, corn and sweet potatoes. Mr. Landreth reports that his crop of oats is more valuable than any other crop, while sweet potatoes exceed the others in quantity raised. He has not had much experience with fruit. Mr. Landreth is fortunate in being able to say that he has never had either a partial or complete failure of any crop, which perhaps accounts for the fact that averaging one year with another, his farm has paid a good profit on the investment.

In common with other residents of the Coast Country, he finds that school and church privileges and social advantages are all that could be desired, while the cost of living is cheaper than in the northern states.

The home market consumes the entire product of his land, and prices, as a rule, are good.

To quote Mr. Landreth: " I consider Southern Texas a very healthy country. Myself and family have enjoyed better health since coming here than for a number of years in Iowa. Had throat trouble in Iowa and am almost free from it now. Would recommend this section for persons of small means if they are willing to hustle. The chances of acquiring a competence with limited capital are far better than in any of the northern states."

E. Leming Mr. E. Leming is one of the small landowners at Alta Loma, Tex., coming here from Nebraska two years ago. His fourteen acres of ground is one-quarter of a mile from the station. Twelve acres are under cultivation; about one-half set to trees and grape vines, with an acre of asparagus. His orchard has not begun to bear yet. Mr. Leming reports that a slight freeze damaged his cauliflowers last November, otherwise crops have been successful. So far his little farm has not become a dividend producer; but he makes a living off of it. Taxes reasonable; schools fair. Home market does not consume all that he raises. Has shipped long distances by express and sold at good prices, but profits were considerably reduced by the transportation charges. Shipments by freight were a losing venture.

The general health of Mr. Leming has improved since coming to Alta Loma, and he can work with more comfort than in the North, except for a few days in midsummer, when the wind blows off the land. Finally, Mr. Leming advises that new settlers coming here should bring with them enough means to keep them for a year or two until the land can be brought into a proper state of cultivation.

O. P. Martin The 518-acre ranch of Mr. O. P. Martin, four miles from Pearland, has not yet been entirely opened up to cultivation. He now has 80 acres planted to cotton, corn, potatoes, peanuts and garden truck. Oats and hay are his most valuable crops. Mr. Martin has not yet engaged in fruitraising, has never had a failure and his products always yield a fair profit.

He finds good local demand for everything he wishes to market.

"A person of small means," writes Mr. Martin, "can secure a home in this section easier than any other place I know of. Have never had better health than since coming to Pearland."

C. H. Patterson

Mr. T. H. Patterson, of Arcadia, Tex., came to Texas from Kansas. He is located within one mile of Arcadia and has been here five years. His holdings consist of ten acres of prairie land, all under cultivation. Mr. Patterson's best crops are grapes, berries and potatoes. The crops mentioned scarcely ever fail, and prices realized are sufficient to yield a fair profit, averaging one year with another. His land is exempted from taxation until 1900. School and church privileges and society are of the best. He has at all times been able to dispose of his products in Galveston at good prices. The shipment of berries north has proven profitable. Mr. Patterson is of the opinion that this is the best climate he ever experienced, and he has been in nearly all the states. Ten acres, in his judgment, is enough for the average truck farmer and fruit raiser.

A CAPE JESSAMINE FIELD OF TWENTY ACRES.

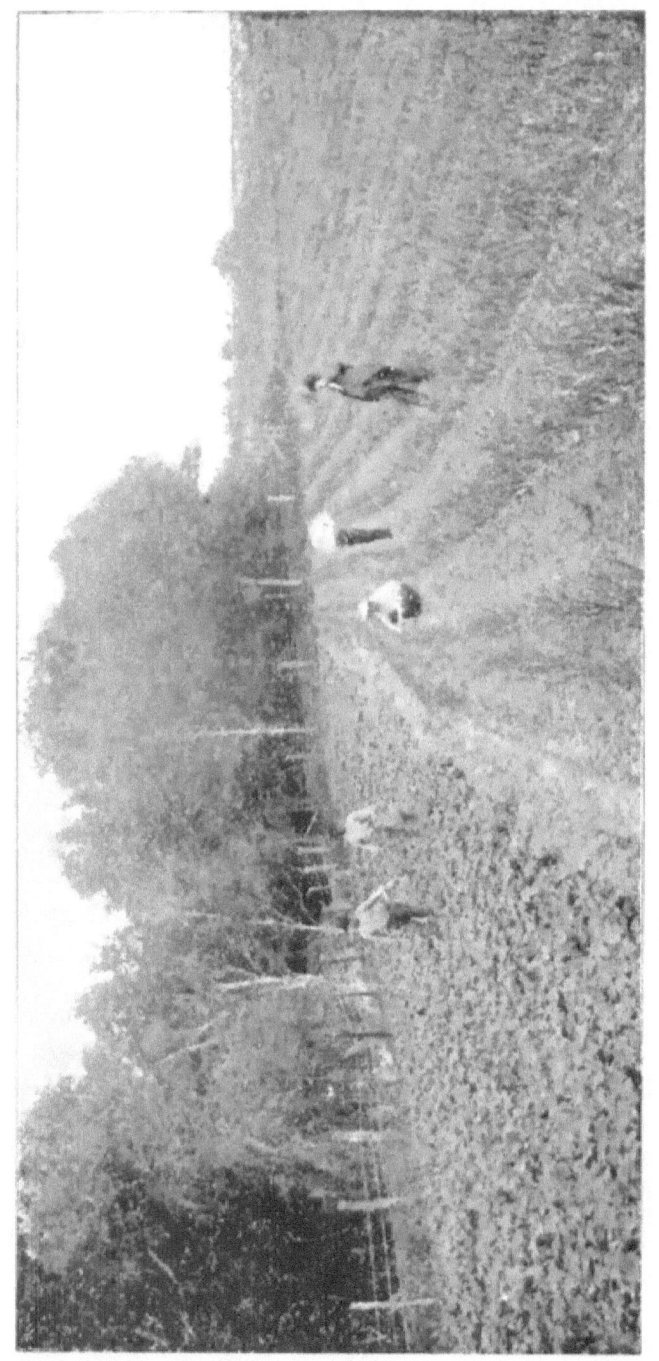

STRAWBERRIES OR ONIONS? TAKE YOUR CHOICE!

Aaron Peters Mr. Aaron Peters, of Fort Bend, Tex., a member of the Mennonite Church, from South Dakota, bought 205 acres of good land at $10 an acre in the Fort Bend Colony. Each 100-acre tract has timber and water on the back end of it. He has already built a house and stable, at less than half what they would cost in Dakota. He is plowing his lands for trees and will have an orchard all put out by spring.

Mr. Peters' family has had good health since coming to Texas four months ago, and a great many of his friends and neighbors in Dakota are coming down this year to share the pleasant climate with him.

He pertinently inquires why his Mennonite brethren should stay north, where what is raised during one-half of the year is used in feeding for the other half.

S. N. Richardson
Mr. S. N. Richardson came to Alvin, Texas, from North Carolina seventeen years ago. He owns twenty acres of sandy loam land within two blocks of the Gulf, Colorado & Santa Fe depot at Alvin. He raises pears, strawberries, peaches, plums and other fruits, flowers, corn, oats, garden vegetables and nursery stock. Pears, after they begin to bear well, are his best crop, running 500 bushels to the acre and increasing in quantity after the trees are eight years old; average price to date more than a dollar per bushel net. Cape jessamine flowers and plants are also leaders with him and pay well. Can grow 40 to 50 bushels of corn to the acre, and vegetables *ad libitum.*

Mr. Richardson's pear orchard is eleven years old, and he has had no trouble thus far in disposing of product. Has also grown strawberries for a number of years with fine returns, crops being sure and sale certain. Peaches and plums have not been so profitable. Grapes have yielded fair returns. He thinks the Japan persimmon and fig are the coming fruits of this section. There has never been a complete failure, and never less than half a crop has been harvested.

Prices of vegetables depend on the time of marketing. By getting in early, satisfactory prices may be realized. Crops must be planted to mature before competition of interior points is felt. If a man is awake to opportunities and takes advantage of them, he will make money. Planting season lasts for the whole year.

State and county taxes are $1.10 per $100 valuation. School and church privileges are good. Alvin and the adjoining country neighborhoods have excellent educational and religious facilities.

The home market takes some produce, but bulk of it is shipped north. Mr. Richardson says he has shipped fruit and vegetables as far as Chicago and Denver by express with good success. Shippers are now mostly using fast freight in carload lots. He thinks a foreign market for fresh pears will soon be a necessity, unless facilities are afforded for evaporating or otherwise disposing of the large product.

"I came here for health," says this gentleman, "and have had it. There is no climatic disease and a man can work the year round. This is a fine country for a rustler, but a lazy man is not at home here, for to succeed at the truck and fruit business requires energy and brains. Many men of small means have settled here and succeeded and there is room for more."

W. H. Thomas

Mr. W. H. Thomas, of Alta Loma, Tex., owns one of the largest farms in the vicinity, consisting of over 50 acres sandy loam. He came from Colorado three years ago and located one mile southeast of Alta Loma. Forty-five acres are under cultivation and set to an orchard of pears and plums, with some grapes. The best crop in quantity is sweet potatoes; in value, corn and peanuts.

Mr. Thomas has not raised much fruit as yet. While there has been a partial failure in some of the crops, it was not complete. Prices are fair, and he is satisfied with his investment so far. Home market does not consume all that can be raised. Shipments of vegetables to Colorado have brought moderate returns, with better prospects for the future.

"I think the climate here in the Coast Country is No. 1," says Mr. Thomas. "Have found nothing to prevent one from continuous work. Further, I believe that settlers with funds enough to get a start, can with industry do very well here, providing their home experience has been along the line of raising small fruits and vegetables."

W. H. Thornton Mr. W. H. Thornton, of
Pearland, makes a specialty
of general truck farming and strawberries. His
sweet potatoes yield heavily and bring good returns
if handled properly, although strawberries and
blackberries are perhaps the best paying crops.
The weather has always been just right for Mr.
Thornton and his crops have never failed.

Living expenses and taxes are low. The local
market takes all that he raises. He advises that
extra early fruits and vegetables be shipped long
distances, as the high prices cover all risks of freezing, etc., but for crops that mature at other times
the nearer home they can be disposed of the more
there is in it for the grower.

Mr. Thornton has no fault to find with the climate
and invites industrious settlers of small means to
come to the Coast Country.

L. D. Troyer The following interesting letter
from Mr. L. D. Troyer, of Fair-
banks, Tex., a member of the Mennonite church,
formerly of Missouri, but for over two years a resi-
of Harris County, gives briefly his experience in
the Coast Country, and his reasons for leaving the
North. The communication is dated January 11,
1898 :

" I removed from Cedar County, Mo. to the Coast
Country of Texas, for the reason that my wife was
told by her physicians that she must seek a better
climate, or die. I also had been afflicted with
catarrh for several years. We came to this Coast
Country two years and a half ago. Today my wife
is a well woman and I am entirely cured of
catarrh. No money could induce us to go back
to the North to live, as the climate, good health and
a new prosperous country, growing rapidly, holds
out great inducements to me.

" I want to say that this healthy climate, with its
ocean breezes, and the good water found everywhere, has given us both a new lease of life, and
several of my neighbors have come here and are
equally well pleased.

" The Mennonites, who have already located five
colonies in the vicinity of Houston, have made no
mistake in this removal, nor in selecting the Santa
Fe as the official route. With the deep water ports
just opened, and immigration from the North steadily

increasing, the good lands and rich soil of South Texas will make our industrious, Mennonite church people, not only a good living, but a competence: and at the prices land has been bought for them there is hardly a question but that it will double in value within the next two years. Their investments here in lands are so much less, while their profits are so much greater, (on account of being near markets and deep water ports) than in the North, that they will continue to be as they now are, entirely satisfied with the change.

"Another point which I deem important: Vegetables, melons, fruits, as well as grains, (all of which do well here) should be shipped in carload lots, and our people grouped together as they are, can arrange to plant so as to ship in that way and receive the largest amount of profits from their labors. They can raise in the late fall onions, cabbage, celery, potatoes, cauliflower and other vegetables, so as to ship them North in carloads early in the spring, where they will find a bare market. Then, in the late summer, another crop for the late winter shipment to the North. In this way they will make it extremely profitable. Our Mennonite people will raise a large acreage of melons this year on the sod.

"These dark sandy loam lands around the city of Houston, are rapidly being settled up, and I can assure my Mennonite friends of a warm welcome by those of us who have preceded them, as well as from the southern people. They certainly appreciate their coming, as all wish this country settled up by such a worthy, honest class of people."

STEM OF KEIFER PEARS.

Pear Orchards
* * *

SUCH is the importance of the pear industry of the Gulf Coast of Texas, that a special article must be devoted to that topic.

Le Conte Pear

The Le Conte Pear is supposed to be an American seedling from the ancestral Asiatic pear, which, in its own home, is an immense forest tree, often attaining the age of 300 years. The original Le Conte tree is still standing in Georgia, a magnificent specimen, hardy, beautiful and prolific. These wonderful new pears are as hardy as forest trees, of luxuriant foliage, grow to a great size, are here free from blight, and yield every year an enormous crop of fruit which sells in Eastern and Northern markets at prices that compete with the older and better known varieties. As a fruit for canning, drying or preserving, they are acknowledged as unequaled. When picked somewhat green and ripened in cellars, many connoisseurs pronounce them equal to the famous Bartlett.

The Le Conte of the Coast Country is the earliest pear grown anywhere in the United States. It can be placed upon the market during the latter part of June, which is fully three weeks earlier than fruit can be plucked in California. The Le Conte is a very fair eating pear; while it does not rank as high as some varieties or command the highest prices, it is a pear that supplies the market, patronized by the middle class. The Le Conte is a very rapid grower, and yields abundantly; in fact it is subject to over production, which must be guarded against. More than 9,000 bushels of Le Conte pears were shipped from thirteen acres of nine and ten year old trees in H. M. Stringfellow's orchard at Hitchcock, during 1893, and the subsequent product has been marketed in equally large quantities.

A Coast Country orchard of Le Conte and Keifer pear trees, upward of ten years of age, properly attended to, should yield a certain annual revenue of $300 to $600 per acre above all expense of taking care of the trees and cost of marketing the fruit.

J. J. SHIRLEY'S PEAR ORCHARD, ALVIN.

Other Varieties

On the Gulf Coast of Texas there has rarely been a failure of the Le Conte, Keifer and Garber pear crop, while in quality the fruit grown in more northern climes suffers in comparison. The Keifer is grown for home consumption. The Garber is better adapted for shipment.

Mr. J. J. Shirley, of Alvin, reports that about 70 to 100 trees are set to the acre, and at ten years old they produce 5 to 10 bushels of pears to the tree. He has one Keifer tree ten years of age, which last season yielded 17 bushels, worth $20; also one Le Conte tree at ten years yielded 16 bushels, for which he got $15. These were his best trees, and should not be taken as a standard by which to estimate average proceeds. Last season

Texas buyers paid $1 per bushel for the pears, boxed and put into the cars at the point of shipment.

Mr. Sampson, near Alvin, has 23,000 pear trees, and many orchards run from 2,000 to 10,000. The Garbers ripen shortly after the Le Contes are through bearing, say early in August. After the Garbers the Keifers begin to ripen, between September 1st and 10th and continue to bear until about the middle of October. The Garber ranks as one of the choicest of eating pears. The Keifer is best suited for canning and preserving. Other varieties grown are the Bartlett and Smith's Hybrid. A few years will find whole train loads of pears being shipped north. At present quite heavy sales are made in Northern Texas, Indian Territory, Kansas and Nebraska. From $1 to $1.25 per bushel is realized.

Texas pears may be canned, preserved, evaporated or made into cider and vinegar. The profits are certain and adequate.

The Profits

That fruit culture pays is evidenced by the following statement of profits realized by owners of pear orchards in the vicinity of Alvin. The figures are gleaned from an article published in a recent number of the local paper at that point.

The Boher orchard of twelve acres (poor improvements but first-class trees) was bought by Mr. Lawler over two years ago for $5,000, and last fall Mr. Lawler sold it to Mr. Haley for $7,000. Mr. Boher paid $12.50 per acre for the land and only cultivated it four years. In that period he made expenses from vegetables grown between the tree rows. The $5,000, less $150, was clear money.

"Fairy Land," owned by Mr. McDonald, 40 acres, only about half in orchard, sold two years ago for $12,000.

Dr. Fehrenkamp paid $8,000 for 51 acres adjoining Major Durant's.

The John F. Durant place of 35 acres sold a year ago for $7,500.

The Nesbit orchard of 20 acres sold three years ago for $3,250.

The Zychlinski orchard of 36 acres was purchased for $5,000.

Mr. E. D. Carter paid $2,250 for his orchard of four and one-half acres.

Prof. J. J. Shirley bought 50 acres twelve years

ago for $6 per acre and refused $16,000 for his
orchard over two years ago. He has a large family
and they have made a living from the vegetables,
strawberries, etc., grown on the place.

Mr. Henry Sampson has 163 acres which he purchased some six years ago for about $10 per acre.
On this he has 19,000 pear trees besides other fruits.
He says he would not take a cent less than $40,000
for his orchard.

Mr. G. H. Cook has 26 acres, on which he has
been living
some ten
years, and
besides
growing
one of the
finest orch-

GATHERING PEARS AT ALVIN.

ards in this section he
has made money and a
name as one of the most
successful strawberry
growers. He refused
$6,000 three years ago
for his place.

The editor concludes by saying: "If you would
establish an orchard and do not wish to do the work
yourself, all that is necessary is to buy the land (say
20 acres) at $25 per acre—which would be $500.
Expense of plowing same will be $50; fencing, $75;
buying and planting 2,000 pear trees, $200. Here
we have an outlay of $825, or half as much for ten
acres. After this is done, there are plenty of good
men who will contract to take the land and care for
the orchard for what they can make on it."

Miscellaneous Products

• • •

Grapes Grapes are planted, cultivated and marketed on the Texas Coast just as they are in California, except that the vineyards of Texas bear no comparison in area with the great grape-growing regions of the Pacific Coast.

Enough has been done from which to form an opinion as to the profitableness of the industry. Leading horticulturists declare that a Texas vineyard, intelligently located and planted with the right varieties, is a certain source of wealth.

The vines are staked and trained to a trellis.

The following grapes grow here in a perfection that no country on earth can excel: Chasselas Muscat or Muscatelli, Chasselas Rose de Peru, Emperor, Black Morocco or Tokay (both flame and white), Malaga or Chasselas Napoleon, Black Spanish, Lenoir or Black Burgundy, Goethe, Rogers No. 1, Salem, Rogers No. 53, Niagara, Black July, Roulander, Delaware, Missouri, Rissling and Herbemont.

If well fertilized, most varieties come into bearing the second year, and when three years old may be counted on for a yield of ten to fifteen pounds of luscious grapes to the vine, and much more as they increase in age.

The Herbemont, Black Spanish and Niagara have proven themselves to be the most successful varieties, as much as $200 net having frequently been obtained from two acres of Niagaras from one crop. The common American varieties all succeed here.

Strawberries Strawberry growers variously estimate their net average yields at $200 per acre. Plants ordinarily come into bearing several weeks earlier than further north, and shippers have the advantage of high prices in markets that can only be supplied from the coast.

Strawberries can be set as early as September, but October is the safest month, and even as late as November the plants will make a fine crop the next spring.

As to profits given out by actual growers, the figures have a Munchausen look; but they are facts nevertheless. One reliable grower shows by his sales book a total of $1,100 sales from less than one acre. Another reports $700 from barely half an acre. The growing of this berry for market rivals in profit the culture of the pear, and the acreage is steadily increasing. It brings in a fair return the first year after planting. You don't get gray-haired waiting

IN A FIELD OF STRAWBERRIES, MARCH 5TH.

for results. Beginning with raw prairie, an acre of strawberries will have cost, to break, harrow, plant, fertilize and cultivate, about $70. The net return next year should not be less than $200, and the same each of the following years. The best results are secured by resetting plants annually.

A prominent grower of strawberries at Alvin states that during March he and his three boys picked from one-eighth of an acre, seven and a half twenty-four-quart crates of strawberries and shipped them to Denver, where they sold for $$ per case, which was $60 for the lot. This was new land and the first crop off of it.

Vegetables The cauliflower will, in the near future, be raised in large quantities for shipment in carload lots. A salt atmosphere seems to be essential to the perfect development of this vegetable, and as the soil here is well adapted to it, every condition is favorable to its growth. It is strictly a fall vegetable, and when sown early in July, and set out in August in rich soil, the bulk of the crop can be marketed before January.

Cabbages, when planted at the right time, yield large returns. There is scarcely a limit to the quantities that can be disposed of in the Northwest, when grown in sufficient numbers to warrant carload shipments. Big crops are raised at Bolivar Point.

The Creole and White Queen onions are as successfully grown here as around New Orleans. They mature in April, just when northern onions are sprouting, and the demand is unlimited at $1 per bushel.

The tomato is another crop that will head the list for profit. It is safely demonstrated that the tomato will produce abundantly in the Coast Country. It begins to ripen May 20th, and at once finds ready sale at high prices all over Texas.

Irish potatoes do well everywhere; the early planting rarely brings under seventy-five cents a bushel in season. Beans, cucumbers, squashes and watermelons are grown in limited quantities.

Rice Texas is fully equal to Louisiana for rice growing.

To insure a good rice crop, two factors are essential: a level body of land, and an abundance of water. In Louisiana water is largely supplied by pumping from water courses with steam pumps. On the Texas coast it can be had from artesian wells at no cost other than the boring of the well.

To plant an acre of rice the first time will cost $15. This includes fences, ditches, levees, plowing and planting. After the ground is once prepared, subsequent planting may be done for $8 per acre. Planting season is from latter part of April to last of June, and crop is ready for harvest in five months from time of planting. It is harvested and threshed very much the same as wheat, and yields from fifteen to twenty-five barrels of rough rice per acre, worth $2.00 to $4.50 per barrel.

A prominent rice planter of Liberty, Texas, reports receipts of $3,700 from eighty acres in 1893, and the entire expense only $500, a net profit of $27.50 per acre. If the rice straw is compressed into bales, and sold for feed, it will pay the cost of the rice crop.

Rice is being extensively cultivated in Liberty County, and is now being introduced into Brazoria County.

This industry is now in its infancy in Texas, but the farmers, realizing that some valuable crop must take the place of cotton, which hitherto has been raised in too great abundance, are turning their attention to rice culture with much favor.

Some of the advantages of rice culture over wheat are: (1) The long period during which the ground can be prepared and the grain sown. Preparations can be carried on from October until June, sowing from March until July, and harvesting extends over a period of nearly four months, from August to November, inclusive; (2) the greater value of the product; (3) the yield per acre, which is from eight to twenty barrels of 162 pounds each.

The prices of rice range from $3 to $4 per barrel. A great deal of money can be made in a few years in rice cultivation.

A FIELD OF SUGAR CANE.

Sugar Cane

There is money in sugar cane. One million acres of south Texas land is suitable for its production. As a matter of fact, only 15,000 acres are devoted to this industry (a paltry percentage) and yet in 1895 the Texas sugar crop sold for $1,500,000, an average of nearly $100 per acre. Seventy dollars an acre may be reasonably counted on, one year with another, one acre of ground turning off 20 to 50 tons of cane, marketable at $3.00 per ton.

Hitherto it has taken a big capital to run a sugar plantation, because in addition to raising the cane it was necessary to change it into sugar in one's own mill. The man with a plow and a mule, however industrious and foresighted, was barred out for lack of dollars. Conditions are changing rapidly, and capitalists are now erecting large central sugar mills, similar to the central factory in Cuba and Louisiana. The small farmer takes his cane there and brings its value back immediately in cash. By this plan the farmer can grow ten acres or five hundred, and the owners of sugar lands can rent them to tenant farmers. The separation of cane-growing and sugar-making processes is in line with the system of large packing houses that consume the steer and porker.

The annual expense for planting an acre of sugar-cane will not exceed $6 to $8, because planting is only necessary every third or fourth year. To culti-vate cane is not half as expensive as to care for a field of cotton. The hardest part is the work of harvesting. Each individual stalk must be cut by hand, a process requiring time and labor.

Sugar is a remarkable crop in the amount of money it diffuses through labor. It requires much care, much handling and much machinery. It represents a large outlay and brings in a large profit.

Mr. J. H. House, owner of the Arcola Plantation, near Houston, says that his profit per acre per annum in cultivating sugar cane is $80, and that the crop is never failing, though some years it is larger than others.

At Sugarland Ed. H. Cunningham & Co. have one of the largest sugar refineries in the world. The plant represents an investment of nearly $1,000,000. This establishment not only refines sugar, but re-cently introduced a paper mill, the paper being made from the pulp of the sugar cane.

Cotton Everybody knows cotton is king, even in these times of tottering thrones; but everybody does not know that Texas produces from one-quarter to one-third of the crop grown in this country. The annual yield varies from two to three and a half million bales. Houston alone handles over half of the cotton crop of Texas.

The Texas cotton belt is divided by Nature into six districts. The territory along the coast, while not producing as many bales as the central district,

excels it in the number of pounds raised to the acre.
It used to be thought that cotton could not be produced on the open prairie lands. The prairies are
equal to, if not superior to the river bottom sections,
and the first cost of land is much less. The average yield is from three-quarters to a bale and a half
of cotton to the acre. Prairie lands yield from a
half to one bale per acre and bottom lands 50% more.
Cotton varies in price from $25 to $45 per bale.
Mr. W. T. Taylor, of Wharton, affirms that in spite
of the dry weather last season (1897) he raised 600
bales on 750 acres.

Cotton is the Coast Country farmer's monopoly.
It is just as convertible into money as a nugget of
gold. Owing to fertile soil, good climate and intelligent culture, this part of Texas combines maximum
yield with minimum cost. The best results are
reached on small farms, with home labor. Under
such circumstances success is as nearly sure as sun-
rise. The Texas cotton raiser who puts brains into
his business, does not have to wait until old age for
a competency even with the low prices recently prevailing. The cotton planter finds here new land,
splendidly adapted to his purpose. Another advantage is cheap labor. Mexican cotton pickers can be
brought in, who will work reasonably and well.

It is thought that within the next few years the
credit of being the first sea island cotton market of

FIG ORCHARD AND RAMIE FIELD, ONE YEAR OLD, AT CLEAR CREEK.

the world will be transferred from Charleston, S. C. to Galveston or Houston.

Another great source of profit is the use which cotton seed may be put to. Aside from the oil, nothing fattens cattle quicker than cotton seed meal and hulls.

Tobacco Fine cigar tobacco, equal to that of Connecticut or Cuba, is now being introduced at various places throughout the Coast Country and promises ere long to be one of the chief products. The soil is in many places admirably adapted for its cultivation, and as it is one of the most profitable of crops and always finds a ready market, it finds much favor among the planters.

Oranges Oranges do fairly well on the Texas Coast. It is expected that with the introduction of certain hardy varieties from Japan the orange will come to have an established commercial value as an article of export.

Figs Figs grow in the greatest profusion. Fruit-growers who are beginning to cultivate it claim it is the most profitable fruit that can be raised in this locality. Two hundred fig trees can be planted to the acre, which will begin to bear in two years and be in full bearing in five years, and will then yield annually 200 pounds of fruit each, a net profit, when dried and preserved, of $3 per tree.

Plums Texas is the home of the plum. It grows wild in the woods in luxuriant profusion. No less than three kinds of wild plums grow in southern Texas, all of fine quality and marketable. The Japan plum is a comparative failure. The American or Chickasaw variety is a success.

Poultry Any practical man can take ten acres of land, and 600 of the best laying hens, and by raising his own feed clear $1,000 to $1,500 each year, and have his fruit trees growing on the same ground. "Broilers" find a ready market in Houston at twenty-five to thirty-five cents a head.

Dairying The fact that milk retails in Houston at ten cents a quart and butter at twenty-five cents a pound, is enough to show that a practical dairyman, who raises his own feed, can realize fifty to seventy-five per cent. profit on his investment and not work very hard either.

Transportation

The key to the whole problem here, as elsewhere, where a surplus can be produced, is a good, near-at-hand market, with quick transportation to foreign markets. The Gulf counties of Texas are everywhere accessible to Houston and Galveston by rail or water. Numerous streams and bayous are navigable inland for long distances by schooners and steamboats. Several hundred small schooners and steamers daily ply between Galveston and neighboring inland places, engaged in carrying freight. The Santa Fe Route opens up a vast market in north Texas, Oklahoma, Colorado, Kansas City, St. Louis and Chicago. But the best guarantee of good prices is the fact that everything here matures several weeks earlier than a hundred miles inland or anywhere else in the United States, except the south end of Florida and Louisiana. The first half of the crop can always be marketed without competition.

STRAWBERRY FIELD IN THE DICKINSON COUNTRY.

A Review

• •

By Mr. Stringfellow

• •

It is just fifteen years since I moved to Hitchcock to embark in the fruit and vegetable business, and plant the first successful pear orchard in the Coast Country. It may not be uninteresting to take a short retrospect of the past, a review of the present, and a glance at the future.

At that time the total number of residents along the Santa Fe line between Virginia Point and Alvin could have been counted on the two hands. The Houston branch had not been started; the Santa Fe had just crossed the Brazos River on its march to the North, and a single train up in the morning and down at night, constituted the entire service. Hitchcock was the only settlement between the bay and Houston, and Mr. Jno. Sealy, who was president of the Santa Fe, being desirous of locating water works on my tract at Hitchcock, offered to give me 200 acres where Alvin now stands, in exchange for 10 acres of my land; but, as one house then constituted the town of Alvin, the prospect was too lonesome, and I declined the offer, although I let him have the use of the land on other terms.

It seems almost incredible that the short space of fifteen years could have sufficed for the wonderful development that has since taken place. Instead of creeping slowly over an open, wild prairie, and through herds of wandering long-horns at the rate of fifteen or twenty miles an hour, once a day, the traveler now speeds at three times that pace, and six times a day, each way, through an almost continuous succession of orchards and gardens on each side of the track, and hundreds of packages of fruit and vegetables daily leave the various bustling little towns along the road. This rapid change from the prairie-waste, with its sea of waving grass, to fertile fields and cozy homes, has been due almost entirely to the wise liberality and fostering care of the various managements, both freight and passenger, of the Santa Fe Railroad. Realizing that on them rested largely the task of settling up the country, it has been their aim not only to furnish, from time to time, reliable information through agents and printed matter, as to the inducements of the Coast Country for the homeseeker, but they have gone further and offered the most liberal excursion rates over the road, and met every reasonable demand for a tariff that will enable the growers to market their products at a profit.

Of course, in its progress to the present high state of development, Coast Country settlers have had obstacles to overcome in places, and disappointments to bear here as well as elsewhere. Drouth, frost and excessive rains have occasionally worked serious harm; but the length of our seasons, and the great variety of products that can be grown, nearly always allow the growers to recoup themselves on a different and successful crop in case one should from any cause be a failure.

Let us see how the Coast Country now stands. From a few packages of vegetables and berries fifteen years ago, we are now growing and shipping thousands of crates annually, and best of all, have induced buyers from distant markets to send their agents down to purchase the various products on the ground. This is by far the most satisfactory plan. It is by all odds better to put prices down to the very lowest notch of profit (as is being done at the present season) and sell for cash upon delivery at the various depots.

As to the future of this section, there can be little doubt that it has advanced beyond the experimental stage. While lands have shrunk in value from the boom prices of ten years ago, they are now on a substantial and reasonable basis, below which they are never likely to fall. The bottom has been touched, and the present time affords opportunities that are not likely to remain long. But, while lands will hardly go lower in Galveston County, it will be folly to buy largely on credit, expecting to make a living and pay for it out of the ground at the same time. This has been a fatal mistake of many of the early settlers of this section. They came with insufficient means, inflated ideas of profits, and often lacked that real love for the business which is the greatest secret in successful fruit and vegetable growing; without it, losses and failure will quickly disgust the

79

planter for money only, which the genuine lover of the business would have borne with patience and conquered by persevering efforts.

Prices of all fruits and vegetables have now come to bedrock all over the country, but if they can be grown with profit anywhere, it can be done here.

In addition to this, we have a most delightful and healthy climate, and the most progressive and liberal railroad in the country, and if a man has made up his mind to change his home (while, of course, it is a serious move) he should give the merits of the Coast Country of Texas a careful examination before taking the step.

H. M. STRINGFELLOW.

STRAWBERRIES PICKED ON CHRISTMAS DAY.

The
Diversified Interests of Texas
• • •

Extracts from an interview with Mr. Jas. A. Davis, Industrial Commissioner of the Santa Fe Route, which appeared in the *Chicago Daily Record* of March 14, 1898:

"Texas, with its area of 270,000 square miles, is an empire richer in itself than Chicago and the West generally begin to appreciate. Within that area are greater diversities of products and more pursuits are possible than in a similar area in any part of the world. Cotton is, and will, of course, continue to be, the chief staple product. It is evident from last season's experience that cotton can be grown there more profitably than anywhere else. The wheat area is rapidly being enlarged, and many flouring mills are now operating in the state and using only Texas wheat. Tobacco is being successfully cultivated and additional lands are being used for this purpose. Sugar manufacturers, too, are finding practical and profitable possibilities in sugar lands in the southern portion of the state. The pine-timber interests are some of the largest in the country, the output for 1896 having aggregated 400,000,000 feet. For farmers Texas offers an exceedingly good field for the cultivation of small fruits.

"For high-grade wools Texas is considered by experts to be second only to Australia. Texas cattle are known all over the United States. Oil has been found in paying quantities, and there are indications of new coal fields.

"The manufacturing interests of the state are increasing and the field is now open to many new industries. The local conditions for such are exceptionally favorable, there being an abundance of raw materials close at hand. The average prosperity of the state is high. The farmers are all greatly encouraged and are engaged in studying the diversification of crops and the possibility of reducing the cost of raising cotton and wheat by giving attention to other farm products. There is a section of the country on the San Angelo branch of the Santa Fe where wheat and cotton are raised side by side on the same farm.

"The towns in Texas are growing rapidly. Galveston, Houston, Belton, Temple, Weatherford, Cleburne, Fort Worth, Dallas and Gainesville all show signs of increasing prosperity. The advantages of Galveston as a port are becoming better known every year, and it promises to be one of the leading ports in the country. Chicago and the west are considerably interested in the development of Galveston's port facilities, as in some measure offsetting any monopolistic tendencies on the part of the Atlantic ports."

PICKING BEANS ON CHADWICK'S PLACE.

Successful Tobacco Culture

● ● ●

The following article is contributed by Mr. W. B. Slosson, of the Houston Newcomers' Association, Houston, Texas, under date of March 18, 1898:

"Please advise the world that the purest and best of Havana tobacco has been, and is now being grown, in at least six counties of the Coast Country. This innovation of transferring the raising of that high-priced staple to southeast Texas is of great interest to newcomers from the North.

"Last year 600 acres of this tobacco was raised. 1898 will see from 9,000 to 12,000 acres grown. The market price of ordinary tobacco is from seven to eleven cents per pound. The price paid to our Texas farmers for Havana tobacco was from fifty cents to one dollar per pound. The duty on Havana tobacco is $1.35 to $2.00 on wrappers, both of which can be raised and handled here as cheaply as common tobacco heretofore raised.

"On February 26, 1898, a meeting of the Texas Tobacco Growers' Association (A. R. P. Moore, of Houston, president) was held at the Houston Business League. At this meeting, Mr. S. J. Washburn, Vice-President of the DeWitt County Tobacco Growers' Association, said: 'We could dispose of 20,000 cars of this tobacco in a single season. There is no limit to the demand for fine cigar tobacco. We have the climate and the soil to grow to advantage light tobacco from Havana seed, and in only a small portion of the United States can these grades be raised. New England and New York are nearly driven out of the market already, for the reason that we can grow better grades for less money.'

"Messrs. Mitchellson & Hubbard, of Kansas City, leaf tobacco dealers, offered me one dollar a pound for some specially high grades that I raised last year. Although I am familiar with tobacco-raising in Missouri, Wisconsin and Ohio, I am sure better profits can be had from raising it in southeast Texas than any other part of the Union.

"Owen Smith & Co., of southeast Texas, sold their crop of 60,000 pounds at sixty cents a pound.

T. J. Rountree produced, last year, 13,000 pounds from eighteen acres, selling 10,000 pounds at fifty cents and the remainder at twenty-five cents.

" The absence of severe winds here is a large factor in tobacco culture. The cheap lands, the high duties on imported tobacco, the long seasons, a large rainfall and an equable climate, makes this Coast Country of Texas especially attractive to settlers who desire to diversify their crops.

" In a state like Texas, where nearly all the staple grains are raised successfully (a state which also raises *one-third* of the whole cotton crop of America), where *all* the vegetables and fruits do well and find a ready market, where the lowest freight rates by both rail and water prevail, coupled with the fact that good, rich prairie lands with plenty of timber can be had on favorable terms at from $5 to $8 per acre—and the reason is apparent why immigrants are now seeking the Coast Country of Texas in preference to any other spot in the Union. And they are coming on every excursion train of the Santa Fe Route; thousands are coming in annually. Those who come (I say it as a formerly northern man) are sure of a cordial southern welcome at all times to this bright land of sunshine and of flowers."

CULTIVATING HORSE RADISH.

What One Man Has Done

In the *Saturday Review*, Galveston, April 16, 1898, appears an interesting article by Mr. Richard Spillane, entitled, "The Story of a Coast Country Experiment." It takes the form of an interview with Rev. J. J. Shirley, one of the pioneer fruit and vegetable growers at Alvin. Extracts from the most valuable portions appear below:

"How much land have you in cultivation?" I asked.

"I have," said Mr. Shirley, "something over 2,000 pear trees. Those trees you see there are the first I planted. Of the 2,000 in the orchard between 800 and 1,000 are now bearing. Year by year I have extended my orchard. The trees over there to the west are young. A few years more and they will bear. I have, all told, 44 or 45 acres in cultivation. Over there to the southwest I have peaches and plums. The big cabbage field you passed as you came up toward the gate is mine."

"What has been the result in a financial way from your farm and orchard?" I asked.

"I have not," said the reverend gentleman, "kept what you would call a set of books, so I can only answer in a general way. While my orchard has been growing, I have grown strawberries, corn, cotton, sweet and Irish potatoes, cabbage, okra, English peas, beets, turnips, radishes, celery, onions, vegetable musk, sugar cane, sorghum, squash, watermelons, canteloupes, red pepper, and dozens and dozens of other things in the rows between the fruit trees. Every month in the year I have been kept busy sowing and gathering some crop. You know we raise two or three crops a year here on the same land.

"When I came here, as I tell you, I had $485. Well, I have paid for my land and I have bought more land. I have spent $2,000 in improvements in the way of houses. I have raised my family. I have sent my sons to Georgetown University and had them educated. I sent my daughter to Granbury College. I've had money in bank."

"Have you had any offers for your farm?"

DOWN THE PATHS OF PEACE

" Yes, many. I should think I've had one hundred or more. The largest amount offered was $16,000 cash."

"And you wouldn't sell?"

" No," was the clergyman's reply.

" Mr. Shirley," said I, " there has been a great deal of discussion about this fruit country between Houston and Galveston. Some men have failed ; some have been successful. Will you tell me—you should be in a position to know—what is necessary for success?"

"Any man," said Mr. Shirley, " who is willing to work and who has a little money to back him up until he gets started can succeed. Brains—good common sense, I mean—muscle and money mean success in this Coast Country. There is more in the man than in the land. Some men are adapted by nature for fruit growing and for gardening. Some men have the power of adapting themselves to it. Some men would make a failure on any land. Any man who is at all practical can come into this Coast Country and, if he had enough money to carry him over the first two years, he ought to run along like a top after that."

" How much land should a man take?"

" I do not think a man should go over 30 acres. He shouldn't work more than 20 acres. He should have a little pasturage."

I asked the Rev. Mr. Shirley to tell me what had been the monetary return to him from the various crops he had raised.

" It's difficult for me to tell you exactly," he replied. " Take strawberries, for instance. Some years I grow a good many of them, two or three acres, maybe. Other years I grow only an acre. The crop and the price vary. I think it would be conservative to put the monetary return of strawberries at $250 an acre. They need a good deal of attention, you know.

" Snap beans ; that is a good crop. They pay from $50 to $60 an acre. I raise them in the spring and after gathering the crop I put the land into cotton.

" Of cotton I raise a bale to the acre on open ground and half a bale to the acre when I plant it between the rows of fruit trees.

" Corn goes 20 bushels to the acre.

" Sweet and Irish potatoes I grow between the

rows in the orchards. Of Irish potatoes I raise from 50 to 75 bushels to the acre. Of sweet potatoes I raise 100 bushels.

" Cabbage is a winter crop. I plant in October and harvest in January, February and March. Last year my return from cabbage was $100 per acre.

" Okra grows magnificently in this country.

" English peas are particularly adapted to this soil and pay well. I make $100 an acre from the crop I sow.

" Beets do well, but I haven't grown many.

" Turnips are profitable. Rutabagas and spring turnips grow as well here as any place in the country.

" Radishes—they are simply prolific.

" Celery is destined to be one of our great crops, I believe. This is essentially a celery region and where proper attention is given the crop is as fine as anyone could desire.

" Onions require a great deal of care and when it is given we have excellent crops.

" I have experimented with rice, with vegetable musk. with sugar cane and with sorghum, and the result has been good. The yield from sugar cane has been 300 gallons to the acre. The sorghum is fine.

" It is needless, I presume, to tell you what a great region this is for squash, watermelons, and cantaloupes. To grow watermelons or cantaloupes no preparation is necessary further than to turn over the sod."

" Now," said I, "tell me about the pears, the peaches and the plums."

" I am growing two varieties of pears—the Keiffer and the Le Conte. Both are successful, but my orchard will not show as good returns as will those of other orchards in the Coast Country. My orchard, from the fact that it is the oldest in the Alvin district, has been the place to which visitors have made pilgrimages. Not only that, but, from the fact that it was the first to bear, my neighbors have come to me to examine the fruit. I have always allowed visitors or my neighbors to help themselves to fruit, so, you see, the yield will appear smaller than it really was. I think one-half of the crop each year has gone in the way I explained.

" The Le Conte trees begin to bear when six years old. The Keiffer bears when four. The first year my trees bore fruit they averaged—that is, I sold—one-half bushel of pears to the tree. I got $2.00 per bushel. The second year the trees bore, or, rather, I sold, at the rate of one bushel to the tree. This year I will sell about five bushels to the tree."

"How much do you get per bushel for pears?"

"I expect at the least $1.00 per bushel. Those I sell in small lots I believe will bring $1.50 per bushel. Those I ship will bring $1.00 per bushel."

"How about plums and peaches?"

"Peaches grow finely here, but the trees are short lived. After bearing three or four years the trees die out. The same applies to plums. Figs are profitable and easy to cultivate."

"Do you make use of such pears as you do not ship away?"

"Assuredly. I have made pear cider here that my neighbors buy and when I let the cider go to vinegar, I have no trouble selling it at 25 cents per gallon. I am about to build a cider press that will turn out three barrels a day. I am going into the vinegar making business, and have no doubt the worth of the article and the purity of the making will create a demand that will support the industry."

I asked Mr. Shirley if he thought there was any danger when all the pear trees in the Coast Country got to yielding that the market would be glutted.

"Gracious, no!" he replied. "Why, some gentlemen from London, who were here, and who were asked what they thought about it said the city of London could consume the entire fruit crop of this region.

"You see, we fruit growers have made a good many mistakes heretofore. We are only now learning our business after having been in the crucible of experience. Formerly we didn't know exactly the proper time to pick the fruit or exactly the way to ship it. Now we have our eyes open. We know something about cold storage, too. And we know where and when to ship."

"What have been the elements that have militated against the Coast Country?" Rev. Mr. Shirley was asked.

"Drainage has been one of the great drawbacks," he replied. "That we are overcoming slowly, but surely. Irrigation is another. It will not be many years before we have these problems solved. Everything we do is for improvement; every season we are nearer to success."

IN A SWEET POTATO FIELD.

Making a Living in Texas

● ● ●

The following extracts are taken from a recent interview in the *Galveston Saturday Review*, with B. F. Johnson, of Arcadia, Texas., President of the Gulf Coast Agricultural Association :

"I haven't got any patience with a man who asks me if a farmer can make a living in this coast country," said Captain Johnson. "Back in New York state they think they do great work if they gather sixty-five or seventy bushels of potatoes to the acre. Here we can raise from one hundred and twenty-five to nearly two hundred. This is, beyond doubt, the greatest potato and cabbage country on the face of the globe. And just remember that when you harvest one crop you can go right along and put in another. There is hardly a day in the year when I can not ship something to market. This farm of mine is only four years old. It looks as if it were eight or ten, doesn't it? Do you see how well drained it is? I came here the 20th of March, 1894. This was then virgin prairie. One of the first things I did was to ditch the land. Then I put in five good drains through my fifty acres. Since then I've worked. Oh! you've got to work in this coast country.

"The crops of vegetables that we can raise are marvelous and the prices we get for our products are about the highest that are paid. We can get our produce to market so early that we get the cream of the trade. I've got fruit growing, as you see, but, goodness gracious, when a man can raise one hundred and fifty bushels of potatoes to the acre and can gather his crop within ninety-four days of planting, and can get from $1 to $1.75 a bushel, what's the use of talking about fruit? And just look at those rows of cabbage. Did you ever see anything finer in the world? This is a paradise for the cabbage grower.

"I have eleven acres in Irish potatoes," said Mr. Johnson, "and from the first lot I shipped I got $1.60 a bushel net and they ran more than one hundred and fifty bushels to the acre. I have nine

and one-half acres yet to harvest and my Irish potatoes should net a good sum this season. Did you
ever see finer cabbage than in that field? I believe
it is the best I ever raised. I have eight acres in
cabbage.

"I have three and a half acres of Creole onions,
fifteen of watermelons, twelve of canteloupes and,
after I harvest my Irish potatoes I'll put that same
land into sweet potatoes. I have one and a half
acres of tomatoes, one acre of tobacco, a patch of
okra, some sweet pepper and a few other things. Of
fruits I have small strawberry and blackberry patches
and am raising some grapes. I have a hundred
peach trees from which the prospect is good of
handsome profit this year; four hundred burbank
plums that are now full of fruit; two thousand five
hundred pear trees which should bear a small crop
this year; two hundred quinces, and some apricots,
soft shell almonds and Japanese walnuts.

"Now, one of the main drawbacks of the coast
country has been the lack of drainage. Just look
around this country here and see what we are doing.
Would you think this had been one of the wettest
seasons we ever had? Know the reason? Ditches.
A few years ago we'd have been drowned out if we
had as much rain as we've had this spring. But
you see we are draining the country. We're not
digging as many ditches as we'd like to, but every
day in the week and every week in the year the
work of improvement is being pushed. The drainage is getting better every day and the public roads
are being bettered."

The farm owned by Captain Johnson is just on
the top of the ridge between the watersheds of the
Dickinson and Hall bayous. Part of the farm
drains into one bayou and part into the other.
Although the land looks to be as flat as a pancake,
Captain Johnson told me there was a fall of nineteen feet in the three and a half miles from his farm
to low water mark in Hall's bayou.

Other Texas Counties

• • •

Below is given a very brief resume of the various Texas counties traversed by the Gulf, Colorado & Santa Fe Railway, excepting those near the Gulf coast which are fully described elsewhere.

In view of the general plan of the pamphlet, which is to call special attention to the Gulf coast section, a complete "write-up" cannot be furnished here. But even this condensation may convey some idea of the immense resources of inland Texas, an empire in wealth and power and possibilities.

Austin County

Population 20,000; county seat, Bellville, population 1,500. Well watered by Brazos River, also Mill Creek, East Bernal and other creeks. Along Brazos River and Mill Creek are forests of oak, ash, elm and black walnut; fire-wood abundant everywhere. Area of Austin County, 700 square miles; one-third under cultivation and two-thirds fenced. Soil is a black, sandy loam in the river bottoms; a black, sticky quality on the prairies and one-third sandy black in hills. Principal crop, cotton; corn and oats also raised and every variety of vegetables. Population mainly a prosperous class of Germans. Best of educational advantages. Summers are never oppressive, while winters are short and mild. Cyclones have never visited this section, and a total failure of crops is unknown.

Bell County

Population about 50,000; county seat, Belton, population 5,000. Well watered with four rivers, numerous creeks and springs; also many fine artesian wells in and around Belton. Timbered with oak, pecan, cedar, etc. Gold and silver found in small quantities in the hills. Area of the county, 1,045 square miles, two-thirds under cultivation. Soil is of a black-waxy nature; about one-third timber land mixed with sandy gravel. Principal crops are cotton, corn, oats, wheat, hay and sugar cane. Various industries: flouring mills, cotton and oil mills, cotton gins, compresses, canning factories, stone quarries and brick yards. One of the most fertile and wealthiest counties in Texas. Plenty of cheap lands from $3 to $20 per acre. The abundance of cotton and wool at Belton affords a fine opening there for cotton and woolen manufacturing. Pleasant winter and summer climate. Never colder than 20° above zero in winter.

Bosque County

Population about 18,000; county seat, Meridian, population 1,500. Well watered by Bosque and Brazos Rivers, Steel's, Spring and Meridian Creeks. Artesian water easily obtained anywhere from 500 to 900 feet. Fuel and fence posts can be had from the timbered land. Soil is a black-waxy quality, except on the rivers where it is sandy. Principal crops are cotton, corn, wheat, oats, rye, barley, millet and sorghum; also all kinds of fruits are raised. The residents are a prosperous class of people. Hot summers, but always a cool breeze; mild winters, very little snow and ice. Land is cheap.

Brown County

Population 17,000; county seat, Brownwood, population 5,200. Watered by Colorado River, Pecan, Bayou, Jim and Ned Creeks. Land well timbered. Area of county, 1,100 square miles. Two hundred thousand acres under cultivation. Soil, a chocolate loam. Crops consist of cotton, corn, wheat, oats, sorghum, millet, fruits and vegetables. Farmers and merchants are prosperous. Very temperate climate all the year round. Rich, productive lands at $4 to $6 per acre on easy terms.

Burleson County

Population 15,000; county seat, Caldwell, population 1,500. Land is watered by Brazos and Yegua Rivers and Second Creek. Plenty of timber. Area of the county, 1,000 square miles, about one-third under cultivation. Soil, sandy black. Principal crop is cotton. Summers hot, winters cool and damp.

Coleman County

Population 7,000; county seat, Coleman, population 2,800. Well watered by Colorado River, Center, Hords, Jim, Ned, North, Pecan and Bayou Creeks. Plenty of timber for fuel, also large coal deposits in southern part of county. Area of Coleman County, 1,290 square miles; one-sixteenth of it under cultivation. Black prairie land; sandy soil in parts of the county. Principal crops: cotton, wheat, oats and all small grains. Cattle, horses and mules are raised in large numbers. Gulf breeze makes the summers cool, while winters are delightful. Climate cannot be excelled for healthfulness. Lands are cheap; county is being rapidly settled. Schools and churches located in every part.

Collin County

Population about 35,000; county seat, McKinney, population 6,000. Land watered by numerous creeks. Large quantities of Osage orange, oak and hemlock timber. Area of county, 30 square miles, four-fifths under cultivation. Black-waxy soil. Crops consist of corn, cotton, wheat and oats; stock-raising is also followed. Principal industries are cotton and oil mills. County thickly settled by thrifty, law-abiding, prosperous farmers. Churches and school-houses in every community. Land in cultivation sells from $20 to $30 per acre. Summers are warm, average temperature 96°; winters mild and pleasant, seldom any snow or ice.

Cook County

Population 40,000; county seat, Gainesville, population 11,500. Watered by Red River, Trinity and Clear Creeks, and other streams. One-half the county is timbered land. Area, 933 square miles. Soil is black-waxy, sandy and red sandy. Principal crops: corn, wheat and cotton. The citizens are prosperous. Gainesville, the county seat, situated on the Trinity River, is a busy city; has eleven churches, six brick school houses, two flouring mills, an ice factory, an iron foundry, a cotton compress, a broom factory, soap factory, cotton seed oil mills, pressed brick works, four newspapers, three banks. The Santa Fe Railway shops are located here.

Dallas County

Population 90,000; county seat, Dallas, population 64,224. Well watered by Trinity River and three tributaries, also small creeks. Plenty of timber, building stone and fire and pottery clay. Area of county, 900 square miles. About 165,000 acres under cultivation, or seventy per cent. of tillable land. Soil of all varieties from sandy to heavy black-waxy. Principal crops: cotton, corn, wheat and oats. Market-

95

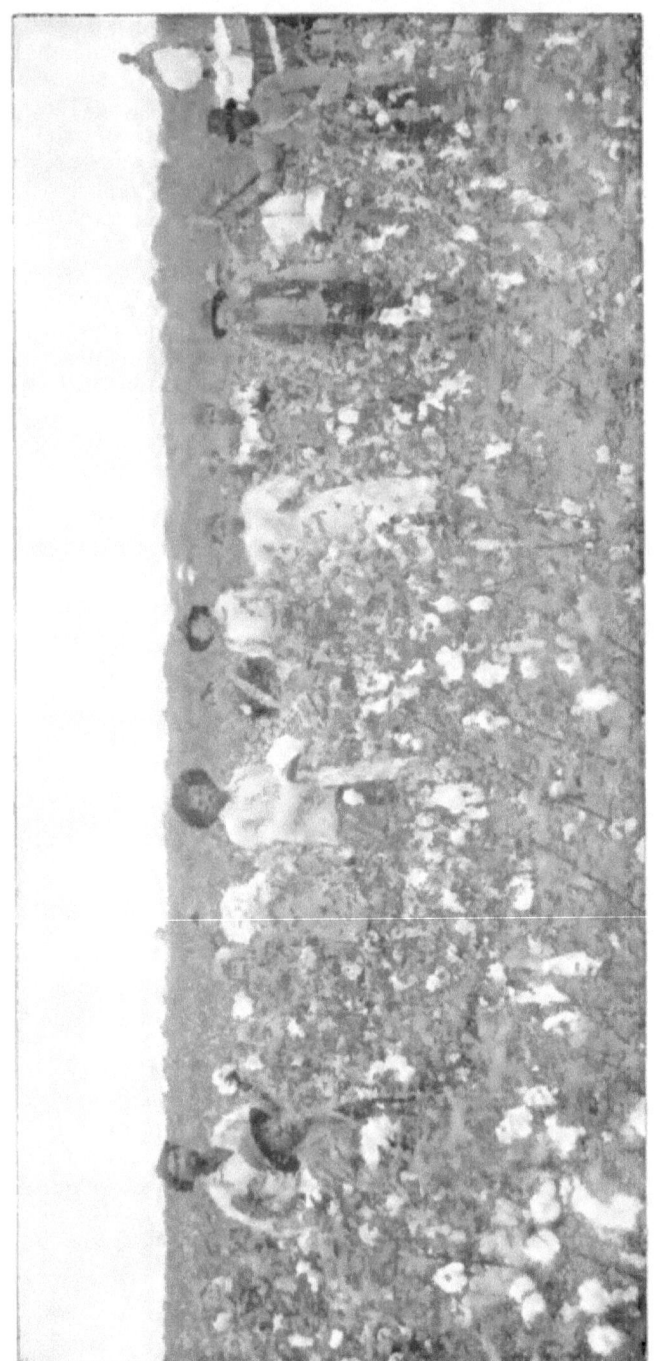

WAY DOWN SOUTH IN THE LAND OF COTTON

gardening and fruit-raising have developed to great extent; also profitable dairy and stock industries. Dallas is largest manufacturing city in state of Texas. The settlers are industrious and prosperous. Climate mild both summer and winter. Farming lands for sale at moderate prices. Unusual opportunities for manufacturing industries.

Delta County

Population 12,500; county seat, Cooper, population 2,000. Plenty of hardwood timber. Area of county, 290 square miles. Eight hundred small farms in Delta County. Soil, black and very rich, from four to fifteen feet deep. Crops: corn, cotton and alfalfa. Farmers and merchants prosperous. Winters mild, summers warm and dry. Land can be rented for from $4 to $5 per acre, and bought for from $20 to $30 per acre.

Denton County

Population 40,000; county seat, Denton, population 5,000. Well watered; artesian water can be obtained at from 300 to 400 feet. Timber in the eastern part of the county. Area of Denton County, 900 square miles; about 100 square miles under cultivation. Soil sandy and mixed with black land. Principal crops are wheat, oats, corn and cotton. Finest wheat belt in Texas extends from Denton west; is about twenty miles wide, and this year averaged between twenty and twenty-five bushels per acre; stock raising and shipping is carried on to considerable extent. The settlers are a thrifty, prosperous people. Mild summers and pleasant winters.

Ellis County

Population 65,000; county seat, Waxahachie, population 7,000. Land watered by Trinity River and artesian wells. Along the streams there is timber sufficient for fuel. Area of county, 950 square miles, three-fourths under cultivation. Soil is a black-waxy quality. General crops: hay, corn, oats, wheat and cotton. Farmers are prosperous. Climate, mild.

Fannin County

Population 60,000; county seat, Bonham, population 5,000. Watered by Red River, its tributaries and springs. Plenty of timber along water courses. Area of county, 1,080 square miles, half in cultivation. Soil, black and waxy; along the river it is sandy. Crops are cotton, corn, oats, hay, wheat and garden products of all kinds. Settlers are unusually prosperous. Climate is mild, averaging from 68° to 75°. Fannin County is noted for the quality of her cotton, which frequently sells for higher price than that of adjacent counties.

Grimes County

Population 25,000; county seat, Anderson, population 500. Is watered by Brazos and Navasota Rivers and their tributaries. Timber and minerals are found in parts of the county. Area is 781 square miles, one-half being timbered and the remainder prairie land; 100,000 acres under cultivation. Sandy and black waxy soil. Principal crops: cotton, cane and corn. Mild climate, average summer temperature 95°; winter 60°. Lands are cheap; a good county for investors and home-seekers.

Hunt County

Population 40,000; county seat, Greenville, population 7,500. Well watered by tanks and cisterns; abundant timber. Soil, black-waxy and sandy. Principal crops: corn, cotton, grains, hay, fruits and vegetables. Cattle and hogs are raised. Farmers and merchants are prosperous. Climate mild in winter, and south breeze makes the summers pleasant. Plenty of good, cheap land from $10 to $30 per acre.

Johnson County

Population 19,000; county seat, Cleburne, population 7,500. Watered by various streams and artesian wells; abundance of timber. Area of county, 1,600 square miles; twenty-five per cent. under cultivation. Soil, black-waxy and sandy loam. Principal products consist of cotton, wheat, oats, corn, and cattle. The settlers are prosperous. Pleasant climate the year round, especially in the winter. Land can be bought on easy terms; light taxation, good schools and ready market for farm products.

Lampasas County

Population 7,565; county seat, Lampasas, population 2,500. Watered by Lampasas and Colorado Rivers, numerous creeks and springs. Plenty of cedar and other fuel timber, also valuable pecan timber. Area of county, 858 square miles; about 50,000 acres in cultivation. A portion of the soil first class for farming, some is sandy and clay. Principal crops are cotton and grains. Industries, wool growing and sheep and cattle raising. Residents a very prosperous people. Excellent climate the year round. Fine school facilities; good homes are cheap. Largest sulphur springs in the world are here.

Lamar County

Population 37,302; county seat, Paris, population 15,000. Watered by Red and North Sulphur Rivers, Pine and Saunders Creeks, and other small streams. Water for stock and domestic purposes easily obtained at average depth of 50 feet. Timber abundant along water courses, such as hackberry, elm, ash, oak and hickory, of splendid quality; also pecan and other varieties, including the famous *bois d'arc*. Soil mostly a rich alluvial and black-waxy land, all exceedingly fertile. Principal crops: cotton, wheat, oats, barley, rye, millet, sugar-cane, garden vegetables, also all kinds of fruits. Stock raising is profitable. Exceedingly fine climate; the nights, visited by soft breezes tempered by Gulf winds, are always cool. Area of Lamar County is 900 square miles; most of the land under cultivation. Excellent school houses and comfortable churches.

McLennan County

Population 50,000; county seat, Waco, population 25,000. Watered by Brazos, Bosque, Aquilla and other rivers, also numerous creeks and wells. Timber is abundant; oil is also being developed. Area of the county, 1,083 square miles; half under cultivation. Soil of river lands, sandy loam; prairie lands, mostly black-waxy. Principal crops: cotton, corn, wheat, oats and all vegetables; also berries and fruits of every variety. Farmers and merchants are generally very prosperous. Climate is pleasant, being tempered both winter and summer by Gulf breezes; average temperature for past ten years, 69°. Good homes at reasonable prices.

Milam County

Population 32,000; county seat, Cameron, population 5,000. Land watered by Little River, Brazos River, San Gabriel, Elm and Pond Creeks. Plenty of post oak timber, also fine lignite beds. Area of Milam County, 11,000 square miles; 75,000 acres under cultivation. Soil, black-waxy and gray post oak with clay sub-soil. Crops consist of cotton, corn and oats. Principal industries are oil mill, compress, water works, electric light and ice plants. Both summer and winter pleasant and healthful. Good land, excellent social advantages and fine schools.

Mills County

Population 7,500; county seat, Goldthwaite, population 1,875. Watered by Colorado River, Pecan, Bayou, Bennett, Brown, Lampasas, Miller and Bull's Creeks. Well water can be obtained at from 25 to 100 feet. Half the county well timbered. There is iron ore and traces of silver and coal. Area of the county, 720 square miles; about one-fifth under cultivation. Soil, mixed, sandy and black-waxy. Crops are cotton, corn, wheat, oats, sorghum, millet, potatoes, melons and vegetables; also small fruits. Farmers are doing well and no financial failures among merchants. Climate delightful the year round. A great health resort. An excellent place for those afflicted with pulmonary troubles; no chills or fevers. Lands may be bought at low prices. Good schools and churches in every section of the county.

Montgomery County

Population 13,000; county seat, Conroe, population 600. Watered by numerous running streams. Plenty of timber of all kinds. Deposits of iron not yet developed. Area of county 1,150 square miles; about one-fourth under cultivation. Soil, principally black-waxy and sandy. Best crops are sugar-cane, corn, cotton, potatoes and tobacco; also fruits. Farmers and merchants prosperous. Summer climate with average temperature of 75° and winter 40°. Good lands, exceedingly cheap, on easy terms.

Parker County

Population 30,000; county seat, Weatherford, population 7,000. Well watered by running streams, springs and wells. Plenty of timber and coal. Area of Parker County is 900 square miles; about 125,000 acres under cultivation. Soil, partly sandy loam, black-waxy and black-waxy loam. Crops are cotton, corn, wheat, oats, hay, vegetables and fruits of all kinds. Climate mild in summer (Gulf breeze), variable in winter.

Runnels County Population 4,000; county seat, Ballinger, population 1,800. Watered by Colorado River and several creeks. Some timber and building stone. Area of county is 900 square miles; about one-fifth under cultivation. Soil, a sandy loam. Principal crops are melons, corn, wheat, oats and cotton. Stock-raising is the leading industry. Climate warm in summer with pleasant breeze; winters agreeable.

Tarrant County Population 60,000; county seat, Ft. Worth, population 25,000. Watered by Trinity River and branches; also creeks. About one-fourth of the county well timbered; half under cultivation; one-fourth grazing land. Soil, sandy and black-waxy land. Principal crops: corn, wheat, oats, cotton and all kinds of vegetables and fruits; also pecans. Delightful breezes in summer; winters warm and considerable rain. Good schools and churches. Population is progressive and liberal. Good opportunities to make money by stock-raising.

Tom Green County Population 7,500; county seat, San Angelo, population 4,000. Watered by Concho River and Spring and Dove Creeks; some timber. Area, 1,800 square miles. Soil, a sandy loam. Principal crops: cotton, milo, maize and sorghum; also hay. Warm, dry summers; winters dry and very little freezing weather. Farmers are prosperous. A good country for stock farmers and farming by irrigation.

Washington County Population 30,000; county seat, Brenham, population 5,000. Watered by Brazos River and Yegua, Jackson, New Years and Mill Creeks. One-third timber land, some minerals. Area of county, 600 square miles; 75 per cent. under cultivation. Soil very rich, black-waxy, black, sandy and loam. Crops, cotton and corn. Manufacturing is the principal industry. Climate, mild; average temperature in summer 80°, in winter 38°. A total failure of crops is unknown.

MAP OF
TEXAS COAST
COUNTRY.

Index

●●

BETWEEN
CHICAGO, ST. LOUIS
AND TEXAS.

www.ingramcontent.com/pod-product-compliance
Lightning Source LLC
Chambersburg PA
CBHW032153010726
47493CB00008BA/2681